OTHER BOOKS BY MARTHE JOCELYN

THE INVISIBLE DAY
Illustrated by Abby Carter

THE INVISIBLE HARRY
Illustrated by Abby Carter

THE INVISIBLE ENEMY
Illustrated by Abby Carter

HANNAH AND THE SEVEN DRESSES

HANNAH'S COLLECTIONS

A DAY WITH NELLIE

Earthly
Astonishments

EARTHLY
Astonishments

A
NOVEL
BY
MARTHE
JOCELYN

Tundra Books

Copyright © 2000 by Marthe Jocelyn
First Paperback Edition 2003

Published in Canada by Tundra Books,
481 University Avenue, Toronto, Ontario M5G 2E9

Published in the United States by Tundra Books of Northern New
York, P.O. Box 1030, Plattsburgh, New York 12901

National Library of Canada Cataloguing in Publication

Jocelyn, Marthe
Earthly astonishments : a novel / by Marthe Jocelyn.

For ages 8-12.
ISBN 0-88776-495-9 (bound).—ISBN 0-88776-628-5 (pbk.)

I. Title.

PS8569.O254E27 2003   jC813'.54   C2002-903630-5
                        PZ7

We acknowledge the support of the Canada Council for the Arts and
the Ontario Arts Council for our publishing program.

We acknowledge the financial support of the Government of
Canada through the Book Publishing Industry Development
Program for our publishing activities.

This book is printed on acid-free paper that is 100% ancient forest
friendly (100% post-consumer recycled).

Printed and bound in Canada

1 2 3 4 5 6   08 07 06 05 04 03

For Martha, my found sister,
and for my writing group,
who listened to a hundred versions

Contents

Earthly
Astonishments

Prologue

Where we lived was a little dot of a town called Westley. Everybody knew about me, so some of them could act natural. But even as a child, I knew I was different. You can always tell from the flash in people's eyes that first second. And from the quiet that follows you until you're far enough away to catch a whisper like a mosquito under your collar.

I was seven when my father came up with his clever plan. He'd been reading a circular with a mention of Tom Thumb's fancy house and all his riches stacking up. My father got to thinking how he had the very same cow to sell.

I'm little, you see. I'm shaped regular, but littler, is all. When I was seven, I was a bit taller than the seat of a chair. I grew nearly nine inches in the two years after that. Then I just stopped growing.

That September, Pa thought to set up a tent at the County Farm Fair. The village folk wouldn't pay money

*to see me because they'd seen me all my life for free. But
at the Fair, there'd be hundreds of strangers aching for
something new and peculiar.*

*My ma and pa went to the trouble to dress me up like
a lady. For one thing, I had lace on my bonnet, which I
surely never did before. Mostly they were ashamed of me
and never made me pretty things.*

*But here I was now, inside a tent my mother and I
had sewed together from bed linens. I was perched up on
a stool, and my pa lettered the sign outside:*

WORLD'S SMALLEST GIRL
LOOK FOR A PENNY

*To start with, I was pleased with myself over my new
bonnet and stockings. They were my first lisle stockings.
But the sun came through those sheets like fire under a
kettle and I about burned up, sitting there all dolled up
and fancy.*

*The folks pushed in four at a time, smelling like barns.
They either shook their heads like there was no words to
say or they laughed out loud with snorts and wheezing.
It was close in there, with me on the stool and my
mother on a cushion beside me and all these dull-wits
crowding around.*

*I started to cry, but my ma smacked my palm with a
strip of leather to make me hush. She could count all the
groups of four and the four pennies each time, and she*

wasn't going to let a bit of fuss get in the way of a fortune. My ma and pa never saw so many coins gathered together in one purse.

The end of that first day, my parents were hopping up and down like idiot children. They even bought me a dish of crushed ice with blueberry syrup poured over, which was a real treat. That made it all right for a bit. I said I'd do it again the next day, though I'm sure they didn't ask my opinion.

The next day was worse. It was hotter. And the word had got around, so there was a line way down the grass by the tent. Pa told my ma to pick up her cushion and come outside so he could fit in six people at a time and collect more pennies.

After my mother was gone, folks thought to poke me. They'd push their fingers under my dress to see if I was real. After that happened once or twice, I started to kick, and I landed a couple of good ones.

Then the folks complained to my pa. He came in, all steamy, and said, "You behave or I'll give you a walloping you'll never forget." His pockets were jingling and that was that. I was so mad I hopped off the stool. I picked it up in my hands and swung it at him. That stool was bigger than I was. But that night, he kept his promise. He walloped me until my mother begged him to stop.

And then he couldn't use me at the Fair for the last day because I had a black eye from where his knuckle bounced off my nose, and my face was all swolled up

*from crying. I couldn't sit down either. My behind took
most of the wallop. And my parents were so mad they
wouldn't talk to me, or each other.*

*It was while we were rolling up our bed linens and
packing our things into the cart that Miss MacLaren
stopped by. She'd been in to spend her penny earlier in
the day, but she ended up examining the seams on the
homemade tent and saying she could use a seamstress
with such a dainty stitch.*

*She and my pa had a quiet conversation under a
maple tree, which I pretended not to listen to. He didn't
look at me again after he took her money. Then my ma
got told what Pa had done. She started sniffling, and I
got put into Miss MacLaren's coach. They never said it
was the last time I'd see my mother. And I never said
that I didn't care much anyway.*

IN WHICH We Discover Josephine's Situation

osephine held her breath as she balanced the heavy bottle of ink. She mustn't hurry, or she'd spill. But it was late, so she'd better hurry. Her boot string had snapped when she yanked it this morning. To tie the knot and tease it through the hole took too many minutes. If only the blasted bell kept quiet until she'd finished this worst chore. She still hadn't caught up and it was near to noon.

Don't ring, just don't ring yet. Josephine reached up to put the ink bottle carefully on Felicia's desk. She hauled herself onto the bench and steadied her feet before filling the inkwell. She had to use both hands to hold the heavy bottle and all her concentration not to spill.

The clamor of Miss Finley's bell made her flinch. Ink splashed across the scarred desktop. The bell announced the stampede returning from the music room. Now she was in for it. No time to fetch a rag. She swiped her apron across the drops, soaking up the evidence.

The dreaded girls burst into the room. Josephine was caught, horribly visible on the bench, as if on a pedestal. She slipped down and under the desk, wishing to disappear. A useless effort, she knew at once.

"Eeek!" shrieked Charlotte. "It's a great, ugly mouse!" Her friends snickered.

"No, no! A hairy, horrible rat!" Harriet was not to be outdone.

With a pounding heart, Josephine crept by the jeering students. Passing Emmy, she heard the whispered word, "Sorry." She turned her head slightly to catch the girl's crimson blush of shame. The others jumped away from her as if from vermin. Josephine was tempted to bare her teeth and hiss like a mad cat, but what good would it do?

She sat herself down in the corner, on an upturned bucket. This was the safest place in the school, with a clear view of everyone's back.

Upon the arrival of Miss Finley, the girls took their places and came to order at once. No one wanted to feel the swipe of the pointer across her palm.

Dust danced in the shafts of sunlight that fell across the room, but there was not a whisper of summer breeze. The windows were firmly shut against the sound of horses' hooves and wagon wheels rumbling past in the street. There was not quite enough air indoors to go around, and what there was smelled of scorched porridge and underarms.

Josephine took a deep breath to calm herself and blew damp curls from her eyes. As the lesson began, she picked up her mending.

Josephine was kept on at the MacLaren Academy because of her talent for tiny, perfect stitches. She could hem a sheet or mend a pinafore more neatly and swiftly than anyone ever before employed by Miss MacLaren.

Josephine blew at her hair again. In June, she did not envy Emmy's flannel nightdress as she did during the winter months. It was too hot now to wear anything so warm. She flapped the soft folds to make a breeze for her legs.

Emmy did have lovely clothes, though. Josephine had once made a dress for herself from a skirt that Emmy had outgrown. She could never wear it, of course, for fear of humiliating the donor. And then Old Betsey had found it one day, under her mat, and Josephine didn't see it again.

She sighed and kept stitching while she listened to the teacher drone.

"If the baker used twelve pounds of flour to make eighteen loaves of bread, how many loaves could be made from forty-two pounds?"

Miss Finley peered out across the classroom, but no one raised a hand.

Charlotte's pimpled forehead slowly sank to her desk. Felicia plucked an invisible crumb from her bodice. Emmy's fingers fiddled with the ribbon tying her left braid.

Pudding-for-brains, thought Josephine. Every one of them. She tied a knot and neatly snipped off the thread.

"Anne?" asked Miss Finley, her voice chirping impatiently. "Felicia?"

May as well look for honey at the water pump, thought Josephine. She folded Emmy's nightdress and reached for Nancy's camisole.

"Your parents will be deeply disappointed if this is your level of performance at Parents' Day tomorrow."

The girls moaned. Miss Finley's bony shoulders slumped in resignation.

"Josephine? Can you give us the answer?"

Josephine saw the herd of faces turn as one to glare at her. Felicia, Charlotte, Anne, Harriet, Emmy, Nancy, and Catherine. She felt the blood rise in her neck, heating her cheeks from within. How she longed to leap up and shout the answer aloud! Sixty-three loaves, you nincompoops!

Six pink tongues popped out in unison, all directed at her and all hidden from Miss Finley by carefully arranged postures. Only Emmy kept her tongue behind pursed lips and stared hard at the floor.

"She's not a paying student at this school," Nancy burst out. "She's a servant and should keep her answers to herself!"

The other girls twittered behind their hands and then waited to hear Miss Finley's response.

"I should think you'd be shamed into paying attention to your lessons. A stunted servant girl, a full year younger, can do them better than you!" Miss Finley snarled. The mistress didn't care that Josephine always knew the answer. She cared only that the others did not.

"Josephine!" Miss Finley did not try to cover her ill humor. "Collect the workbooks! Bring me the workbooks immediately!"

Josephine slid her mending into the basket and stood up. She examined her too-big hand-me-down boots, wiggling the bare toes inside.

This was the moment she most dreaded each day. It was a test she performed and failed every morning, with the blood pulsing in her ears. She walked along the row of desks, reaching up to take the book resting on each one.

"Freak!" whispered Nancy.

"Runt!" hissed Charlotte.

Anne's fancy, red shoe shot out at the last second, too fast for Josephine to avoid. She fell with a thud, letting the workbooks fly and slapping her palms on the planked floor, amidst a shower of laughter.

Miss Finley glanced at the grandfather clock against the wall and promptly grasped the handle of the bell on her desk. She rang it sharply, signaling that it was time for the young ladies of the MacLaren Academy to follow their teacher to lunch.

Although Josephine was on duty in the kitchen during the midday meal, she waited on the floor until the students had giggled their way out of the room. She had long ago learned that it was safer that way. If she were foolish enough to show pluck during an incident, another would be soon in coming. Josephine felt lucky today. Incidents in the classroom usually involved an inkwell tipped in her direction.

The trills and warbles of the girls faded away down the hall. Josephine stood up and pulled her apron straight.

If I don't hurry, I'll be walloped for sure, she realized, scurrying to the door. The new cook was vicious with the ladle. Old Betsey had left a week ago to live with her son. Betsey had been in the Academy kitchen for probably a hundred years, certainly the five years of Josephine's stay. She'd had a tongue that could slice an onion, but she never hit. Not once.

Josephine bunched up her skirts and galloped the shining length of marble tile, clattering like a horse bus on Broadway. She closed one eye at the sign reminding her:

RUNNING IS NOT PERMITTED
IN THE CORRIDORS
OF MACLAREN ACADEMY

She paused at the top of the narrow back staircase. Josephine did not like stairs. Each riser came up to her knees. Climbing up and down was like tackling the side of a dangerous gully. Since no one was watching, she clambered to the bottom on all fours like a baby, feeling carefully for each step with her boot.

Josephine could hear the dreadful voice through the kitchen door.

"Where is that puny dwarf?" The cook's bellow was louder than the pots crashing or the squeaking wheels of the service trolley cart.

Sylvester, the scullery boy, grunted his assurance that he didn't know where Josephine was hiding and didn't care a fig.

"I'll give her such a thrashing she won't walk on those stumpy little legs for a week," promised Cook.

Josephine's legs weren't stumpy. They were skinny, if anything. It's Cook who's shaped like a stump, she thought. A stump all covered with knobs.

The bell from the dining hall rang insistently, begging for luncheon to be served. Josephine imagined the cooling lumps of haddock, the boiled potatoes, and the mashed parsnips. The food was all the same blanched white as the crockery it sat upon.

"You'll have to wash your face, boy," said the cook, "and take in the trolley yourself."

Josephine heard a burst of cussing from Sylvester.

"And if you see that lazy pygmy, you tell her I've warmed the ladle."

Josephine sank onto the bottom step. She couldn't think of one reason to push open that door.

2

Josephine
Makes a Decision

It was well after lights-out when Josephine leaned against the ice chest, pressing her sore bottom to its cool side. Through her thin skirt, the ladle had branded moon-shaped welts across her thighs.

Josephine had waited as long as she dared to appear in the kitchen. Sylvester had leered at her over the tea tray and continued to smear lard on the bread. Then Cook silently unhooked her weapon from its place over the fire and closed the oily fingers of her other hand around Josephine's wrist. She had grunted with each whack, sending puffs of curdled-milk breath down Josephine's neck.

Now Josephine shifted her backside to a fresh, cool spot. Old Betsey hadn't thought much of her, but she would never have whacked her with a ladle. Josephine's eyes burned again, as she fought the tears down.

"Nasty hag! Horrible hog!" Josephine couldn't send enough bad thoughts in Cook's direction. And her saying that Josephine carried disease and ill luck!

Suddenly the idea that had been flickering like an ember in the grate sparked a fire in her brain. She would run away! Why stay here for another walloping? Her thoughts began to fly in circles, gathering up speed.

Old Betsey hadn't been so cruel as this cook was. There would be another position for Josephine. Unless all cooks were cruel and Betsey was the odd duck. Was that possible? How could Josephine know? She was small, but she was a hard worker, and she would prove it. But she was small, no changing that. One look and most folks spat. Or laughed. Could she find the right folks? If she walked a ways from the school? She'd knock on kitchen doors until she found a better situation.

She'd need some food. Josephine paced around the ice chest, tapping her knuckles along its side as she made a plan. She'd take Cook's cheese, hidden in a tin behind the cracker barrel. And the bread ends. What about her shawl? It wouldn't be hot always. And money. Josephine stopped moving. She might need money.

The only person she knew with money was Miss MacLaren. The headmistress spoke of money often; especially how much it cost to give the MacLaren Academy girls their fine education and how disappointed the parents would be to find their dollars were ill-spent. A bucket of nonsense, as far as Josephine could tell. The only money being spent was on Miss MacLaren's hats and her tasseled velvet cape, on her chocolates all the way from Belgium, and on the scented cushions in her study. The headmistress must have pockets full of money!

Josephine had never needed money before now. She was fed—a little, and clothed—unless you looked close.

So what did she need with money? But Old Betsey had been paid, Cook got wages, even Sylvester, she supposed, must receive a few pennies, since he kept coming back to plague them all. And Miss MacLaren had promised a wage to Josephine's father that very first day at the Fair! So where was it? She'd have to ask for her pay!

She ignored the sign in the hall outside Miss MacLaren's study:

ENTRY IS FORBIDDEN
TO THE STUDENTS
OF MACLAREN ACADEMY

A gas lamp burned on the wall by the door and another on the gracious writing desk. The walls had fancy paper on them, with a dark, rose-colored stripe. The whole room was pink and ghosty feeling. It was like being inside somebody's stomach.

The headmistress sat hunched over her desk. By her feet was her prayer stool, its hinged lid open to expose a cedar-lined compartment. Miss MacLaren's hands moved in the circle of lamplight, scratching numbers in a book. Josephine hesitated at the open door, her exhilaration dribbling away.

Miss MacLaren's lips hung open slightly while she wrote. Josephine was reminded of the luncheon haddock when it was still whole, lying gape-mouthed on the chopping board. She realized with a jolt that stacked on

Miss MacLaren's desk, just beyond the circle of light, were little towers of coins. The haddock was counting her riches!

Josephine nearly stole away back to the kitchen, but a picture in her mind, of Cook wielding the ladle, forced her across the carpet. Miss MacLaren banged her book shut when she found a face peering up at her.

"Whatever do you mean, sneaking at me like that?" One hand pressed against her floral bodice, while the other promptly shielded her treasure from Josephine's eyes.

"I didn't mean to sneak. I'm quiet, is all." The sound of her own husky voice surprised Josephine; she could go days at a time without speaking to anyone.

"Well? What can you possibly want?"

"I want . . . I want you, please, to pay me. It's five gold dollars. You promised my pa when you took me in. One gold dollar for each year's service, you said. Please."

Miss MacLaren's plump hand slid down from her bosom and smacked the surface of her desk, making a hollow thump. Her words came out like steam from between closed teeth.

"My arrangement with your parents is no business of yours. A creature like you is lucky to have a corner to sleep in and food each day. I'll thank you to never again put me in the position of discussing money with a servant."

She dipped her pen and returned to work, without blinking her stony eyes. Josephine's ears stung, as if the unkind words had scalded them. Her feet stumbled over themselves, backing out of the room.

"Excuse me!" Miss MacLaren's curt bark stopped Josephine in her tracks. "I have not dismissed you. For your impertinence, you will do some copying."

Josephine tiptoed forward again to receive the pages thrust into her hands.

"Ten duplicates by morning. Take ink and pen from the drawer of the hall table. You may go."

Josephine trudged back to the kitchen, trembling with anger at her own foolishness. She lit a candle and crouched on her mat, not daring to rest before she had copied the words:

> *I will behave myself wisely in a perfect way.*
> *This much I can do for Teacher.*

Morning came too soon for Josephine's backside to have a chance at healing.

"What's the trouble, Worm?" asked Sylvester, with a sly look. "Having trouble sitting down?"

"Keep out of my way, and I'll keep out of yours," threatened Josephine. "Otherways, I'll make your eyes grow crossed."

He shot her a look that told her he believed her. His hand flew to his face, as if to protect himself. Josephine laughed to herself all morning, watching him peel potatoes without glancing up. Meanwhile she stayed as far from Cook as she could manage and still complete her tasks. And tasks there were aplenty.

It was Parents' Day. The front vestibule was festooned with flags and ribbons, welcoming families from all over New York City, as well as towns beyond its limits. Certain girls would return home next week, it being end-of-term, while others would remain as summer boarders.

Many parents arrived by horse cab, while some families, like Charlotte's and Emmy's, had splendid carriages of their own.

The Academy choir lined the walk, wearing their new summer boaters and singing, "Onward Christian Soldiers."

Josephine spied through the cellar door onto the street, watching the ladies arrive in skirted coats, with gentlemen in silk top hats. They all paused to smile at the chorus of girls before entering the school and being directed toward the dining room.

Josephine wondered briefly where her own parents were today. Certainly not dressed in Sunday clothes, stepping lightly out of horse cabs. Not visiting their only daughter, bearing gifts of books and peppermints. Not thinking about her at all.

"Hey! Worm!" Sylvester yanked her from the doorway. "Time to serve the high and mighty!"

The kitchen had produced delicacies rarely tasted at MacLaren Academy. The traditional Parents' Day luncheon was a roasted lamb with parslied potatoes and pitchers of gravy and whole gardens-full of green beans. Josephine wondered if the parents were hearing complaints of the usual fare or whether they believed their own bellies.

As luncheon was cleared away, parents were invited into the classrooms to inspect examples of their daughters' work. Miss MacLaren hovered at the bottom of the stairway, directing traffic with a beaming countenance.

"Lovely to see you, Mrs. Hicks! I'm sure you'll find that Felicia's penmanship has improved this term.

"Mr. St. James! It's an honor to have you with us today. A busy man like you!

"Mrs. Montgomery, I hope you'll take a moment to go over the Academy Betterment Fund with me. I know you pride yourself on being a generous contributor."

The afternoon program included Miss MacLaren's speech on the importance of discipline in education, as well as a recitation by the lower school of the poem "The Charge of the Light Brigade," by Alfred Lord Tennyson. Then Josephine could hear the steady intonation of times tables while she laid out the tea things in the visitors' parlor. She liked this room best in the whole school. It was dim and cozy, and even in summer, there was a fire in the grate, crackling a welcome to company.

The hammering of footsteps on the stairs warned Josephine to hide. Usually the thought of spectators would send her scooting down the hall to seek cover in the kitchen. But today curiosity burned fiercely. She decided not to scurry away. She would stay and watch the families.

The door flew open to admit a breathless, thirsty throng. Josephine stood on tiptoes, trying not to rattle the cups as she reached up to place them in gilt-trimmed saucers. No one paid her a moment's attention as they helped themselves to the bounty of cakes.

Miss MacLaren had reminded the girls that this was an opportunity to demonstrate their company manners. The girls, who liked best to scoff and sulk, were curtseying and simpering like society ladies.

Emmy's mother smoothed her daughter's hair. Felicia was fussing about her new gloves being too small. Josephine listened to parts of several conversations.

"Oh, Daddy, do you really mean it? May I ask a friend?" Nancy glanced around quickly. "Anne? Do you want to come with us to Mr. Barnum's two-ring circus on Saturday next?"

Anne clapped in delight, and the two girls retreated to the corner to whisper.

Emmy leaned against her father's shoulder. "I'm happy you came, Papa."

He patted her awkwardly.

"Have you heard anything from Margaret?" she asked.

Emmy's father, balancing his top hat on his knee, looked out the window and shook his head.

"We don't discuss Margaret, Emmeline. Unless you

wish to break your mother's heart. Tell us about your studies. How is the French grammar this term?"

"Oh!" cried Emmy suddenly, jumping up. "I'm meant to be passing biscuits!" She seized a plate of gingersnaps from the table and offered it, trembling, to her parents.

Josephine smiled to herself. Poor Emmy was a cabbage head when it came to French verbs.

"I was particularly impressed with the needlework," Emmy's mother said to her husband. "I had no idea that Emmy was making such progress in her embroidery."

"Oh, that name card was a mistake, Mama," Emmy interrupted. "None of us can sew worth a penny. It's the serving girl who made all those samplers. She's ever so clever. She did the calligraphy too. On the proverbs— Ow!" Emmy's voice ended in a whimper. Nancy had pinched her.

"Nancy! Why did you—"

"Shut your stupid mouth, you fat squirrel!" Nancy hissed at her.

In the silence that followed, Josephine could hear her own heart stop dead. She'd stayed awake until after midnight making display copies for Parents' Day.

Josephine quivered, agreeing with Nancy, for once. Oh, please, Emmy, don't say another word!

Miss MacLaren was unaware, until Nancy's pinch, that anything was amiss. Now she swooped down, like a hungry hawk.

"Girls?" The frost in her voice might have iced the tea. "Whatever can have prompted this display?"

Josephine held her breath.

"Nancy? Emmeline? I'm speaking to you."

"I thought Nancy pinched me," Emmy sulked. "But I guess it was an accident." She rubbed her arm, not trying to hide her pout.

Josephine hated to see Nancy's smirk, though it reflected her own relief.

"I was only saying, Miss MacLaren"—oh, no, Emmy!—"that there has been a mistake. The sewing samplers and the proverbs all have the wrong names." Emmy spoke quickly, as if trying to get it all out without further interruption.

"It was the little serving girl who made them all. None of us could do it half so well. Look, there she is! See, by the table. It's her you should compliment, Mama!"

And Emmy didn't stop there! Josephine did her best to shrink into the draperies, but Emmy came over! And stood there beaming, pointing down at her! Josephine yearned to shrink away completely. Instead, she was the center of attention for the circle of gaping parents and mortified girls.

Miss MacLaren had other plans than congratulations for Josephine.

"Is that the story she's been telling you?" The headmistress sniffed in contempt. "Our little charity case has a lingering problem with the truth," she announced to the audience. "Don't you?" She turned her furious eyes on Josephine. She leaned over to reach Josephine's arm, which she squeezed between her meaty fingers.

"You are excused from the room. We do not wish to see you again."

The seven steps to the parlor door seemed to take seven minutes. Once outside, Josephine leaned against the wall, taking in gulps of air. "She does not wish to see me again?" Josephine clenched her fists to strengthen her resolve. "Well, then, I'll run away is all!" She found herself nearly skipping down the corridor. "She will never see me again."

3
IN WHICH Josephine Takes
What's Hers and Makes a Friend

Josephine feared that Miss MacLaren might send for her, might devise a punishment that would slow her departure. But she was soon forgotten. Josephine waited in the linens cupboard until the visitors were gone and the girls were shepherded to bed.

She dozed briefly, on the stack of wool blankets recently removed from the dormitory beds. She was awakened by the chiming of a clock, but not soon enough to count the bells.

The school was dark and quiet—nearly quiet. There were always creaking boards and window cracks with wind whispering through.

Josephine wasted no more time. She went directly to Miss MacLaren's study and straight to the desk. Where was the money? Where did Miss MacLaren put her little towers of coins when she'd finished counting? The drawers were firmly locked.

Josephine remembered last night's visit and the open prayer stool near Miss MacLaren's feet. And sure enough, the embroidered knee rest lifted easily, revealing a lisle stocking nestled within. It clinked faintly when Josephine lifted it out.

She grinned as she poured the contents onto the carpet of cabbage roses. So much money! Gold eagles and half eagles and gold dollars, all chinking and clattering like a rickety music box playing a beloved song. Josephine sorted them by value, tracing the Indian heads on the dollars with loving fingertips.

"If a nasty woman with squishy arms has twenty-six gold dollars hidden in a stocking," murmured Josephine, "and she pays a long-owed debt to a loyal worker, how many gold dollars does she have left?"

Josephine took one dollar for each of the nearly five years she had lived at MacLaren Academy. She carefully returned the others to their hiding place.

Josephine closed her fists around the small coins and poked her head past the door frame, peering into the unlit corridor. She heard a small gasp and turned her head. Her nose met the nightdress of Emmy St. James.

Had she stood there long enough to see Josephine take

the gold dollars? Josephine waited in silence, clutching her treasure. Emmy seemed to be waiting too, observing Josephine with real attention.

"I was looking for you," Emmy whispered. Her hair, brushed out for bedtime, hung past her waist. "I hate this house at night. It's always creaking and moaning. What were you doing in Miss MacLaren's study?" When she squinted, her cheeks were very round.

"I . . . I . . . thought I heard a noise. May I go now, Miss?"

"I was looking for you. I had to tell you how very, awfully sorry I am. What's your name anyway?" Emmy asked. "The others just call you . . . Well, never mind. What's your name?"

"Josephine, Miss."

"Please don't call me Miss." Emmy suddenly fell to her knees so that her blue eyes could look directly into Josephine's green ones. "Don't call me Miss at all. I'm just a girl, like you. I hate when they tease you, I just never have said, because then . . ."

She turned away and squeezed her eyes shut for a moment. Josephine thought of her in the classroom, always looking at the floor while the others were acting up.

"I have to go now, Miss, I really do." Josephine's fingers were numb, wrapped around her dollars.

"My name is Emmy."

"Emmy."

"Couldn't we, could we, have a little midnight party?" Emmy sounded almost forlorn.

"Oh, Miss." It was a new feeling, being wanted for something. But Josephine couldn't stay here, especially to play, now that she'd made up her mind.

"I got walloped something dreadful today—"

Emmy gasped. "But that was all my fault!"

"I have to leave," Josephine explained quietly, making it real. "I'm running away."

"But where will you go? This is horrible. It's all my fault. Where will you go?"

Josephine avoided the question. "I'm leaving tonight." Her fists tightened around the coins. "So, if you don't mind, Miss, I have a few things to do first."

Emmy stood up.

"We can't go to the dormitory to talk," said Emmy. "We'd wake the other girls. Where's your room?"

Josephine looked at her with suspicion. Could she really not know?

"I don't have a room. I sleep on a straw mat behind the stove."

Emmy gaped. "But that's terrible!" She spoke out loud and then shushed herself with flapping fingers.

"It's quiet," said Josephine. "It's warm in winter." It's better than the flagstone floor. Or a room full of nasty girls, come to think of it.

Emmy turned around abruptly and headed off down the corridor. Josephine leaned over in a flash and slipped the coins down the inside of each boot. They pressed into her ankles, but they made no noise when she walked. Gently she shook the kinks out of her fingers as she followed Emmy to the kitchen.

"How do you see in here?" whispered Emmy. "It's black as black."

"When it's black, I'm asleep." She reached under her mat for a precious stub of candle.

"That's better," said Emmy when the candle was lit.

She poked Josephine's pallet before sitting down.

"There's no crawlers," said Josephine. "I shake it out every day." She had never had a guest before. Emmy's house probably had whole extra sofas for guests to sit down on.

They huddled close to the tiny flame—as if it could warm them.

"I promise I won't tell anyone that you're leaving, Josephine," said Emmy, after a minute of quiet. Her voice was soft and almost admiring. "To make up for the trouble I caused. I wish I could go too. Nobody talks to me. If it weren't for you, I'd be the one to torment. No, no, I know it's true. I'm not very clever and my toes turn in, though I wear my shoes on the wrong feet to straighten them out." Emmy sighed with the weight of truth.

"Sometimes, I've even—I've even said thanks in my prayers that you were here." In the candlelight, it seemed that her blue eyes had filled up with the chance of tears. "I'm sorry."

Josephine felt a prickling high up in her nose. Emmy was the first person who had ever apologized to her, for anything. She sat next to her, close but not touching.

"Where will you go?" Emmy repeated.

"I don't know yet."

"Oh, my goodness!" Emmy gushed suddenly, wiping her eyes and laughing.

"I've just had the best idea. You could go to my sister!" She clapped her hands, making the candle flame waver. "My sister, her name is Margaret. She's eighteen. She got married in October to a man named Robert, but she calls him 'My Bob.' He's the nicest man, with lots of gingery whiskers. I feel a bit sorry for Margaret, having to kiss all those whiskers, but I guess she likes him enough to overcome it. My father hates him. He's a piano player. He plays what my father calls the 'devil's tunes' at a tavern on Ludlow Street called the Half-Dollar Saloon. Remember that name, Josephine. My father said that a half-dollar was more money than he'd ever give Margaret if she threw away her life to marry Robert. Margaret put her hand on her heart and said, 'My Bob is my life!' My mother sobbed and collapsed. She stained the cut-velvet chair with her tears. Jilly, our maid, was crying too. Margaret fastened her best bonnet and said, 'Good-bye, Mama.' My father just looked into the fireplace with his back all stiff, and Margaret walked out the door, but she winked at me first.

"I've not seen her since, but she writes me letters at school. She has to work now, for money. Every day, in a

sewing factory. You could work there too, Josephine.
Your sewing is beautiful. Margaret says there are lots of
children who work there. It makes her want to weep,
she says. She says I'm lucky to be at a good school and
that I must study hard at my lessons." Emmy paused to
think about that. "It's hopeless. I study so hard, I think
my brain will burst, but I don't remember anything."

Above their heads in the visitor's parlor, the grandfather clock bonged the eleventh hour. The candle's
wick sank into a puddle of wax, and the flame died.

"You must go to bed, Miss," whispered Josephine. "I
mean, Emmy, Miss." The coins were digging holes in her
ankles. "You've been real kind tonight, but you're risk-
ing awful trouble."

"Let's pack you a lunch," suggested Emmy. "We're in
the kitchen. You must know where everything is, even in
the dark."

"Cook is very handy at keeping most food locked
away," said Josephine, "but I'll take what there is."

Groping in the blackness of the pantry, Josephine collected the heels of the day's loaves of bread and opened
the tin box where Cook hid the cheese. She was disappointed to find only a small wedge left.

"Look!" cried Emmy. "I tripped over the apple barrel." The skirt of her nightdress was full of fruit.

"I don't need so many!" laughed Josephine. "I intend
to find Margaret and have a stitching job before I eat
even three apples!"

She tucked everything into her apron pockets and reached under her mat to find her needle case.

"Why don't you just go home?" asked Emmy. "To your own house and your mama?"

It was hard to say the words aloud. "It's my parents who sold me here, to Miss MacLaren. They'll have none of me now."

"Sold you?" Emmy squawked like a frightened bird.

A creak sounded on the floor outside the room. The kitchen door swung open with a moan. Cook's scowling face, illuminated by a candle lantern, looked like the mask of a ghoul.

Emmy screamed a scream to be proud of, giving Josephine time to duck into the shadow of the stove.

"Oh, Cook!" burbled Emmy. "You gave me such a scare!"

"What the devil are you doing in my kitchen?"

"Oh, Cook, I was just as hungry as could be. See? I've got myself an apple and I'm going back to bed!"

Josephine was astonished. This was the girl who claimed not to be clever?

Emmy marched past the old witch with the nerve of a soldier.

Cook followed her out, muttering curses.

Josephine leaned against the still-warm side of the stove until her heart stopped thumping.

4

Josephine Moves On

The kitchen door was locked at night, but the key was hung on a string next to it. Getting in might be a problem, but getting out was not.

Josephine dragged over Cook's stool to reach the key. Then she dragged it back beside the table so nothing would be amiss at first sight. Except the fire in the stove would be unlit. Josephine grinned. Breakfast would be late tomorrow.

She used the key and left it on the floor beneath its nail. She opened the door, stepped outside, shut the door behind her, and finally took a breath.

She paused just inside the gates, looking back at the looming shape of the school. She was usually asleep on her straw at this time of night. She had never been outside to see the tall house with black windows under the moon. It had never felt to her like a home. Josephine knew that a home was a place you wanted to go back to.

Suddenly, in the top window, all the way to the left, a curtain shifted. Josephine saw a pale face and two hands press against the darkened glass. She stepped backward as her heart jumped into her throat. The building looked as if it could indeed be haunted, but this waving figure was no ghost. Josephine's breath rushed out in a whimper of relief as she waved back. It was Emmy, saying good-bye.

Josephine stood on tippy toes to reach the iron latch of the gate. She stepped onto Broadway and pulled it closed behind her, with a determined clang.

Clouds floated in front of the moon, so the only light came from a hundred yards down the road, where lanterns hung from poles around the entrance to a bustling establishment. Miss MacLaren had warned her girls many a time about the evils that lurked beneath the sloped roof and cheery sign of The Philosophers' Inn.

Josephine knew that Ludlow Street and Margaret were somewhere downtown. Emmy had said so. Where exactly she could only find out by talking to a stranger. That seemed impossible. She would worry about that later. First she had to get closer.

Perhaps she could walk there, but she didn't know how long it would take. She certainly couldn't walk any distance with five gold dollars making blisters on her ankles.

The fence turned a corner at the edge of the Mac-Laren property. Josephine crouched next to it, just off the street. The coins fell out as she tugged off her boots. She pulled her boots back on and rummaged in her pocket for the sewing case. The moon obliged her by escaping its cloud for a few minutes.

Carefully she set to work, unpicking the row of stitches that held up the hem of her skirt. Beyond her own steady breathing, Josephine became aware of the sounds of night around her: a cricket somewhere nearby, distant cart wheels, and the mournful howling of a dog.

When she had made a dollar-sized gap, Josephine slid her riches into the fold at the bottom of her skirt and then set about sewing a circle around each coin, to hold it safely in place. Stitch by tiny stitch, breath by quiet breath, she completed her task.

Now she was ready. The apples in her pockets bumped gently against her legs as she set off. A wagon clattered by, pulled by an old horse. Josephine stood rigid, afraid to be seen, and then shrank into the shadows. A scraping noise above made her jump. She shook herself. Probably only a squirrel. She mustn't let the night scare her!

She headed toward The Philosophers' Inn, meaning to cross the road before she came too near the abundance of light at its entrance. There was a rowdy cry and a rejoining laugh just before the barking started. She heard more than one dog, suddenly and angrily sprinting in her direction. The doorman at the inn shouted after them, trying to call them back.

Josephine spun around and jumped into the road, feeling the sharp yapping closing in. She knew the beasts were likely bigger than she was. Then, thundering out of the darkness before her, appeared a horse bus, kicking up grit in all directions.

For an instant, Josephine froze, trapped between

attacking dogs and the fast-approaching horses. Then she hurtled toward the darkness and safety on the other side of the road, straight across the path of the oncoming hooves.

The shriek in her head came out as a hiccup. The horses reared back in confusion, snorting foam. The carriage teetered dangerously before coming to a standstill. The dogs howled and raced back to the shelter of the inn.

"What the devil was that?" hollered the driver, jumping to the ground in a fury. Passengers were emerging from the sides of the horse bus, examining themselves for bruises.

"Biggest rat I ever saw!" proclaimed a round man with huge gray whiskers. "Those mutts are lucky it got away instead of staying to fight!"

Josephine, trembling in the shadows, smiled faintly.

"All aboard!"

"Where are you headed, my man?" called someone from the entrance of the inn.

"Straight down Broadway. All the way to the bottom. Last ride of the night."

"Would you hold up an extra minute? I've left my hat."

The driver cursed and spat, but he waited.

Josephine took the delay as an omen of good fortune. She had been watching for her chance. She grasped the step at the back end of the bus and heaved herself up. Instead of boarding, however, she kept her head low and slid into position with her hands gripping the platform and her feet wedged on the wheel brace.

The hatted man took a seat on board. The horses tossed their heads and snickered quietly, quite recovered from their surprise. The driver snapped his whip, and the team lurched into motion. The horse bus, the driver, and the eight passengers within rocked back and forth with every ripple in the road.

One extra passenger clung on behind with all the strength her tiny arms could muster.

IN WHICH She Arrives
at the Half-Dollar Saloon

Josephine rode the horse bus until her bones were rattled into rice. She finally tumbled from her perch during a stop at the corner of Houston Street. She was shaking from ears to toes and covered in the muck that had been sprayed up by the wheels. Weak in the legs, she hobbled her way to the wall of a store called Murray's Feed and Grain and sank to the ground amidst the litter of rags and papers. Her blue dress was as dirty as a dust cloth, anyway.

Close by was a pile of corncobs, leftovers dumped by a sweet corn vendor. A black rat ignored Josephine as he feasted, flicking his whip of a tail.

Josephine's mouth and ears and curls were full of grit. Her curls? Her hand clapped the top of her head. Her cap must have flown off during the ride, and the string tying back her hair was gone with it.

She leaned against the bricks, counting the hours she had been awake. Nearly twenty! No wonder she was wishing for her straw mat. But she couldn't stop here. She had to keep going until she found Margaret and a safe resting place. She pulled herself up and started to walk, avoiding the debris and staying close to the buildings.

"Hsst!"

Josephine nearly jumped out of her boots.

"Clear off!" It was a fierce whisper. "This is our spot! Get gone!"

A footstep away, in a shadowed doorway, lay a boy. No, two boys. The smaller one was stretched across the lap of the boy who glared at Josephine.

"I said, 'Clear off.' " His hand lay over the other's ear, protecting his sleep. Could a boy be any dirtier than this?

"I'm going," said Josephine, soft and sulky. "I didn't see you. I'm tired too, is all."

She noticed a brush and rags and a bottle of bootblack next to him, but his feet were wrapped in sacking, not wearing shoes.

The little boy's smutty cheek nestled against his brother's raggedy breeches. Filthy fingers ruffled his tangled hair.

"I just, I wonder, I just need to know . . ."

The boy seemed not to have noticed her size. His hand caressed his brother's head, but his eyes narrowed when she spoke.

"I have to find Ludlow Street."

He pointed with his chin. "That way."

"Thank you."

She turned to go and then paused. Under the boy's suspicious watch, she dipped into her pocket and took out an apple, keeping the other for herself. She laid it down beside the bottle of bootblack. The boy's stare softened and his hand darted forward to take the prize.

Josephine headed out across Houston Street as a clock pealed the half hour past midnight. A church bell soon echoed the chime. She could see the faint outline of a spire some distance further down Broadway.

To Josephine, the few blocks to Ludlow Street were like ten miles. Despite the lateness of the hour, the streets were humming with trade, but of a kind she'd not witnessed before. All manner of villain seemed out to do business at this time of night. Josephine crept from doorway to doorway, masquerading as a shadow.

She saw dark-suited men and fancy-dressed ladies exchanging bottles and whispers and packages and paper money, all in the open air outside a series of rough establishments. One man descended into a cellar from the street, carrying a writhing canvas sack.

"I've got some fierce rats tonight!" he called out to his mate. "Your flea-bit dog has got a fight ahead of him!"

The stores and buildings in this part of town were huge and stuck right on each other, with no room for grass or trees. There seemed to be a tavern or a grog house in nearly every one. She caught wafts of grilling meat, fried fish, and ale. Rotting foods tossed into the gutter sent up competing smells.

The roads were wide and dotted with the day's garbage and horse muck. For someone of Josephine's size, the piles of refuse were like hillocks, which she clambered over with effort, ever more dejected. At the Bouwerie, she passed under the elevated train tracks, stretching across the sky. In their shadow were many more sleeping children, wrapped in sacking and as dirty as chimney sweeps.

How did so many children come to lose their families? Josephine wondered. Is this where she might end up? Was she loony, thinking she could find Margaret, when she'd never even crossed the street by herself? Well, humph, she'd made it this far, even got a ride! So she wouldn't stop yet.

The thought of sleeping in the street, huddled over a steam vent, gave her the fire she needed to find her destination. The Half-Dollar Saloon was on the street level of a towering house of three or four stories. Tipping back her head, Josephine could scarcely catch a glimpse of the night sky, somewhere above the whole row of such buildings.

The windows of the saloon were bright, gaslit from within, and the sign over the door was cut in the shape of a giant silver coin. Josephine could hear shouted laughter and lilting music. Maybe that was My Bob playing the devil's tunes on the piano. Certainly it had a different sound from the plaintive hymns learned by the MacLaren Academy choir.

There was a single window cut into the door, high up and far out of reach of Josephine's curious eyes. She had no choice but to push open the door and creep through it, without knowing what she might find on the other side.

IN WHICH She Meets
Mr. R. J. Walters

The heat and the smoke and especially the forest of legs were a shock. Josephine looked around in a panic for a hiding place. She slipped quickly under a table and crouched in the sawdust that covered the floor. From there, she could spy out on the tavern.

She'd never seen so many brogans in one room. Men's feet were just enormous! Other than Sylvester at the school and old Teddy Burns who delivered the coal, Josephine was not acquainted with men.

She could hear a violin accompanied by the piano, but her only glimpse of the piano player was a salt-and-pepper beard above an emerald green cravat. Now that she was here, she didn't know how to approach him.

Then the musicians started a new song, and the din of conversation dipped momentarily for the crowd to hear what it was. A couple of men began to sing along amidst good-natured jeers.

Josephine hugged her arms about her knees and closed her eyes with a silent moan. Suddenly a hand touched, then grasped her shoulder. Her heart stopped altogether.

"Hey, you, Missy!" A woman's face, shiny with sweat, was only inches from Josephine's own.

"I thought I saw someone creeping in under there. You're a tiny thing, aren't ye? Where's your dad?" She was coaxing. "He shouldn't have you in a place like this."

She had an accent that spread out her words. She might have been pretty if she weren't so tired looking. Limp scraps of auburn hair peeked out from under a white kerchief. She must work in the kitchen. She wore an apron, and a sodden cloth was slung over her shoulder.

"My dad's not here." Josephine had to lick her lips to make them work. "I came on my own. I need to speak with My Bob." The woman's face was blank. "Robert, I mean. The piano man."

"Robert isn't working tonight. That's Patrick playing now. And Toby, scratching on the violin."

This possibility had never occurred to Josephine. Whatever could she do? Must she wait until tomorrow to find Robert and Margaret?

She noticed her own muddy fingers trembling. She clutched at her dress to steady them and felt the ridges of the coins in her hem. The woman was watching her closely. Josephine evaded her eyes and shimmied backwards a bit. She winced. Her bottom was still tender from the cook's beating.

"You're alone then, Missy?"

Josephine nodded.

"Have ye eaten?"

"No," she whispered.

"You're so little! Ye need supper maybe?"

Josephine nodded. Suddenly it occurred to her that she could pay for supper. But how to cut the coins out of her skirt without anyone seeing? The woman reached for her hand and helped her crawl out.

"Will there be trouble for you?" Josephine asked, thinking what would happen to her if she fed anyone at the school door.

"The boss won't be back except to lock up," the woman promised. "Stay close by me."

Josephine tucked herself against the woman's skirt and followed her down a hall toward the kitchen.

"Ah, Nelly, my dear!" A low voice stopped them. The woman holding her hand bristled. The corridor was filled with the shape of a man, a tall man, wide and burly.

"Good evening, Mr. Walters," said Josephine's companion. "I didn't know ye were with us this evening."

As the man leaned down, Josephine could see his grand, black moustache, reaching from ear to ear.

"You must have work to do, Nelly. Perhaps I can entertain your friend a while." His voice was rich and deep.

He knelt down on one knee, trying to come face to face with Josephine. Briefly, he held his palm flat next to her temple and then moved it to his own chest.

"I was getting the child a bit to eat, Mr. Walters," said Nelly, not leaving easily.

"Then do that," said the fine, big man. "She's hungry, of course. I can see that. She'll eat at my table."

"Oh, no, sir!" Josephine found her voice. Eat with a stranger?

"But I insist!" He smiled at her.

He must use a very strong tooth powder, thought Josephine. Certainly, the whiteness of his smile was tremendous. And his dark eyes were steady on hers. No sign of disgust.

"I'll have a mug of beer, Nelly. Order the child's supper and bring me a warm towel." It was a mild command. "A clean one. Not that foul thing men use at the bar to wipe the beer foam from their whiskers."

Nelly squeezed Josephine's hand before she backed into the main room and disappeared.

The light was dim. The man leaned closer. He smelled clean, like soap, not rank and sweaty the way the coal merchant always did.

"Please, do me the honor." He offered his hand, which could have held six her size. He had promised food. It seemed worth the risk. The woman, Nelly, was still nearby. Josephine let him lead her to a table. He removed his coat and rolled it into a cushion for her chair.

"Thank you," she whispered. He was like a knight, performing an act of chivalry! "Thank you very much," she said more loudly.

"Allow me to introduce myself . . ." The man had a voice like honey! "My name is Randolph James Walters, known to most as R. J. Walters. You have no doubt heard of me?"

Josephine shook her head, then wondered if she should have professed otherwise.

"Well, now that has changed. And you would be?"

She hesitated. Was there any reason not to say the truth?

"Josephine. Just Josephine."

"Well, then, Just Josephine," he said with a wink, "are you on your own? Lost, perhaps, in the big city?"

She tipped her chin to pretend confidence. "I am alone, but I'm older than I look," she assured him. "I'm only here to see a fellow about a stitching job in a factory."

"Indeed!" He smiled again.

Nelly appeared, carrying a towel on a tray. Mr. Walters took it and handed it to Josephine.

"You'll want to clean up a little, my dear, before I get your supper."

Josephine felt a flush of true gratitude as she pressed the warm, damp cloth against her face and then wiped her dirty hands, leaving streaks of filth on the towel.

"I may be able to help you, my dear." Mr. R. J. Walters was speaking now in an undertone. "I've been looking for someone like you."

What could he mean? Josephine's neck prickled.

"Someone who might change my fortune," continued Mr. Walters. "I suspect that we can help each other."

"But what—"

"You're tired now. Tomorrow we'll talk. I will arrange for you to go home with Nelly tonight. Would that be suitable? In the meantime, let me see to your supper."

He rose and headed to the bar. Nelly was at her ear in an instant.

"Is everything all right, Missy?"

"Oh, thank you, Nelly, yes. Who is that man? He's so, so, like a gentleman in a book! He said he'd been looking for someone just like me! That I might change his fortune."

"Ah, did he now?" Nelly finished wiping the table and used the same cloth to wipe her own forehead. "Aye, and he might well believe that to be true."

"Do you think so, Nelly? Because I don't want to let anyone down, or make a mistake."

Nelly's eyes were somehow looking beyond the walls of the dark and smoky room. Then she flashed a smile at Josephine, one that made her tired face seem merry for a moment. She hooked her fingers in the glass beer mugs on the next table and was gone.

Josephine watched Mr. R. J. Walters cross the room, holding a plate of fried potatoes with bacon. He put her supper on the table and tucked his handkerchief around her neck before offering the fork.

7
IN WHICH Josephine Finally
Goes to Sleep

Josephine might have consumed a pipe herself for all the smoke she tasted while waiting for Nelly to finish her shift at the Half-Dollar Saloon.

At the end of it, Mr. Walters insisted on carrying her out. "She can weigh no more than a couple of chickens."

In a wink, Josephine found herself astride the man's shoulders, her fingers clenching the folds of his coat. He must be rich indeed to wear so thick and soft a garment! Her poor worn dress was like tissue paper in comparison.

Nelly lived on Forsyth Street, only a short distance away from the Half-Dollar Saloon. The house was one of those tall, grim buildings that paid no attention to comfort.

"Can you do no better than this, Nelly O'Dooley?"

Mr. Walters complained. His polished boots were picking their way up rubbish-strewn steps. Josephine wondered the same thing. Was Nelly so poor?

"That'd be up to you, now wouldn't it, Mr. R. J. Walters?" Nelly asked gruffly. There was no answer.

"I'll not venture inside." Mr. Walters swung Josephine to the ground. "Sleep well, my dear. Have pleasant dreams."

He turned to Nelly.

"Bring her into the museum in the morning," he said. "We'll settle everything then."

Museum? Did he work in the museum uptown? With the dinosaur bones? Mr. Walters went down the street, adjusting his shiny top hat. Nelly sniffed at his retreating back and put a hand on Josephine's cheek.

"Well, you'll be needing to sleep for a week to get your strength up for what's ahead on your road. Come along in."

Josephine followed Nelly into the tenement. Something brushed past her leg in the dark. She caught her breath and wished right away that she hadn't. The stench in the hallway was that powerful. Someone had cooked cabbage, maybe a hundred times, but that was the kindest odor. There must be cats who lived here and a privy close by.

She didn't like to put her hands down where she couldn't see what they were touching, but Josephine needed help climbing the three flights of narrow stairs. Nelly paused at the top.

"Now, tread quietly through this door. My boy Charley and I have got the back room, but the Wong family live in the front. And there's no light, none at all, until I can get to the candle on our table, so hang on to my skirt and step light."

Josephine did as she was told, trying not to breathe. As warned, there was nothing but blackness. She shuffled along next to Nelly's skirt, which smelled of cigars and beer. In the first room, she could hear someone snoring and a child's cough. How peculiar to be tiptoeing past a stranger's sleep like this.

Through a curtained doorway, they came to a stop. She could hear Nelly fiddling. The match was struck, and the candle lit. Without warning, a pale face rose from the darkness beyond. Josephine cried out before she could stop herself. The boy had white hair and pink eyes.

"Mercy, Charley! You'll send us into fits, popping up like a ghost. What are you doing awake anyway?" Nelly tousled the boy's startling hair.

"You skeered my guts through a hole," said Charley, his voice croaking before he laughed.

He was near as tall as his mother, but white as a bleached bone and skinny, as Josephine could all too plainly see. He was naked from the waist up, and his shoulder blades stuck out like budding wings.

"Put a shirt on, son. We've got company."

"But it's hot as the devil's own oven in here."

Nelly pulled a shirt down from a nail on the wall and handed it to him. Charley slipped his arms into the sleeves, squinting his alarming eyes at Josephine. The candlelight seemed to make his pupils dance, not letting her stare him down.

"So, Nelly, who've you got here?"

"This is—why, Missy! I don't even know your name."

"I'm Josephine."

"Josephine, this is my son, Charley O'Dooley. I can see the two of you have plenty to be googly-eyed about. Charley is an albino. That means born with no color in his skin or his hair or even his eyes. But there's plenty of color in his language, thank you very much."

Charley grinned, giving himself dimples and transforming his unearthly face into that of a rascal.

"And from the looks of things, you're a midget, eh, Josephine? Which is why Mr. R. J. Walters was so on fire to be friendly this evening."

This news shook the smile off Charley's face and tied a thick knot in Josephine's stomach.

"What do you mean, Nelly? He seemed, he was, he said . . ." Her voice trailed away. Nelly was folding her lips to the inside and Charley was picking at a button thread with too much interest.

"It's late, Missy, we should be getting you settled, not all worried up. You'll have plenty of time to see things for yourself in the morning. And if it makes ye feel any better, Charley here works for Mr. Walters too."

"Yeah, and I bring home more money than she does!" added Charley, with an affectionate look at his mother. "But not enough to buy us a palace yet, eh, Mumsy?"

Nelly rubbed his cheek. "Someday, Charley. Someday. Now then, Josephine, we don't have a bed for ye, but I can see from the droop of your eyes that a blanket in the corner will be enough for tonight."

Finally settled, Josephine lay in her appointed corner with her head spinning. The day's hot air was trapped in the room. She needed the blanket more for under than over. How much had happened since she stood in the headmistress's study, planning her escape! She thought of Emmy and the coins in Miss MacLaren's stocking and the cook's face in the morning when Josephine would be noticed missing. She thought of the bootblack boys, curled in their doorway. She tried not to wonder what Mr. R. J. Walters was planning for her.

She listened in the dark to the breathing so close by, trying to distinguish whose was whose. How lucky she was to meet Nelly! Then she realized, as she faded into sleep, that as odd as they might be to the rest of the world, she and Charley were two of a kind.

8

IN WHICH Josephine Visits
the Museum of Earthly Astonishments

The crimson banner over the arched doorway
on the Bouwerie was lettered in gold:

R. J. WALTERS' MUSEUM OF
EARTHLY ASTONISHMENTS

Josephine's oversized boots dragged to a stop so that
she could look at the colorful posters nailed to the pillars
in the shadow of the elevated railway tracks.

ROSA, THE LADY WITH A BEARD
AS LONG AS SAINT NICHOLAS!
HALF MAN, HALF ALLIGATOR!
SEE FOR YOURSELF!

"That's me," said Charley, hooking his thumb at the
painted likeness of a chalk-faced ghoul. " 'Charles, the
Albino Boy! A Ghostly Phenomenon!' Bleeding lovely,
aren't I?"

Josephine stared from the boy to the picture and back
again. This is how Charley worked for Mr. Walters? Her
shoulders went cold.

The boy leaned so close that his floppy, white hair

tickled her cheek. "Don't look so queasy. It's better than flogging buns or newspapers like every other lunkhead, getting your feet wet all the day long." He put his hands on Josephine's shoulders and peered at her with his darting pink eyes. "You'll do fine, little one. Think of it as being in the theater. That's what I do."

"You run along now, Charley. Get yourself to work. Mr. Walters'll be in a fine pucker if you're late again."

Charley ducked his mother's kiss and then saluted as he ran inside.

"That's where the staff and the paying customers go in," Nelly explained. "His Nibs is the next door over. Oh, and Missy? Be sure to find out the fee he's got in that greedy mind of his. You're worth twice times, or more, whatever he says."

Without another word, she escorted Josephine all the way to the center diamond in Mr. Walters's office carpet. Mr. Walters bounced to his feet when they came in and rubbed his palms together.

"Did we sleep well?" He bent over Josephine to ask, as if the mood of the day depended on her answer.

"If she's staying on with us, she'll be needing a mat, sir." Nelly was quick to the point.

"We'll all be moving to the summer quarters in Coney Island on Saturday. I'm sure a bed will be found at the boarding house. It is nicer for all of us to be out of the city for a few weeks. Thank you, Nelly, for bringing her in this morning. You can wait in the main hall."

Josephine lifted her head with a jerk. "I want Nelly here," she said quietly.

"Indeed?" Mr. Walters swallowed that like a sour cherry. His eyes narrowed, and he sat down on a wooden chair to look at her.

"I would like you to join our little family, Josephine," he said quietly. "But first we need to know a few important statistics."

He stood up and produced a folding measuring stick seemingly from nowhere.

"With your permission?"

She could feel her lips tightening as she held back squawks of anger. Should she let him? Could she stop him? Should she kick him? He held the stick against her back. She could feel the warmth of his large hand as it rested for a moment on her head.

Mr. Walters made a little noise in his throat, like a bumblebee deep inside a daffodil. Josephine caught a look from Nelly's eyes that made her sharpen up.

Maybe she should wait to see what he offered?

"Just as I thought!" He exclaimed, his smile nearly as wide as his moustache. "Under twenty-nine inches! Well under twenty-nine inches!" He beamed at Josephine, as if expecting her to marvel with him.

"How old are you, my dear?"

"Twelve last October."

"Twelve? Hmmm. Perhaps we could say fourteen? Or fifteen? To make it even more, even more . . ." He patted his pockets and then riffled papers on his desk until he'd found a small notebook and a pencil. He began muttering to himself and making notes.

"New clothes, of course, right away, first thing, and shoes! Do those clodhoppers fit, my dear? No, I didn't think so. Take them off, let me see your feet."

Josephine's cheeks were burning and her hands were like ice as she yanked at the knotted laces. If nothing else good comes of this, she thought, at least I'll get a pair of real shoes, fitted to my own feet and not stuffed in the toes with crumples of paper.

Mr. Walters crouched next to her, like a giant bear. He seemed hardly able to wait for her bare toes to emerge, as if he would eat them up and lick his lips after.

"Your feet are four inches long! Four inches! I am delighted, my dear, simply delighted!"

Nelly's eyebrows were raised, maybe laughing to see this huge man in his fancy suit down on the floor. Josephine's shame suddenly floated away, and she felt a burst of hope inside. She had something that Mr. Walters wanted, and Mr. Walters was a rich man. She was good at arithmetic. She could make up any sum she wanted.

"I am prepared to offer you room and board, and new dresses, plus ten dollars a year, in exchange for your services in our museum," stated Mr. Walters, his voice steady and warm, as if promising the moon. "What do you say to that, my dear?"

Josephine could hear the clock ticking with a steady, hollow click. Tick, tock. Must talk. Tick, tock. Must talk.

Having learned the carpet pattern by heart, she lifted her chin to face him.

"Mr. Walters." It came out in a whisper. She cleared her throat and tried again. "Mr. Walters. When I saw those pictures out front, I was ready to skedaddle straight to the stitching factory. Then I remembered you bought me my supper, and Charley said it wasn't so bad here anyway. So I thought it wouldn't hurt to hear what you had in mind.

"But I'll need more than what you're saying." Josephine didn't know where her courage was coming from. Maybe from Nelly's soft smile over in the corner.

"First of all, I want to be where no one can touch me. Up somehow, so they can look, but no touching."

Mr. Walters smiled. "Of course, my dear, I can understand that. You shall have a platform, all your own."

Josephine raced ahead before she could succumb to the jitters. "And I want two gold dollars every single week I stay with you, and I want it paid on Saturday night, not saved up for someday later on. Every week."

Mr. Walters jumped back to his feet. Josephine could see Nelly's jaw roll open and knew she'd overstepped it.

It was amazing how a voice could change from honey to grit in the wink of an eye. Mr. Walters began spitting his words, as if they were bits of stone.

"Perhaps you have forgotten that you are a gutterpup. Do you think life for a freak in a garment factory will be a merry one?"

Josephine's heart plunged to her four-inch feet.

"I am taking a tremendous risk," Mr. Walters continued, "by investing in you at all. What if you start to grow? What then?"

Josephine's eyes stung, her tears making a sneak attack. She looked at Nelly, feeling hopeless. Nelly winked. That was all Josephine needed.

"I don't think I've got any more growing to do, sir. But I suppose you can't be sure of that, not knowing me. I guess I'm pretty small, anyhow, even if I did grow a little. Mr. Barnum, who's got the new circus? He might think I'm small enough, being under twenty-nine inches and all. I might try going to him before I go to a stitching factory." She stopped talking and listened to the clock.

Mr. Walters clasped his hands and bowed his head, as if in prayer.

"Josephine," he said finally, "I will accept your conditions."

Josephine pinched herself to stop from laughing.

"If you start to grow, our arrangement is over. Is that understood? You are a tough little thing, but it adds to your charm. I foresee a prosperous partnership between us." He turned to Nelly.

"Nelly? I can trust you to clean her up for tomorrow? She's a bit ripe."

"Aye, sir."

But Josephine wasn't quite finished. "Mr. Walters? Because Nelly found me and will be looking out for me, she gets a half-dollar extra every week.

"Those are my rules. You can say yes or no."

Next morning, when Nelly suggested a scrubbing, Josephine wasn't quite sure what she meant. Why, she'd washed her face and hands the night before last in the Half-Dollar Saloon. Surely that had taken care of things for a while?

"No, Missy, I mean your whole body, and your hair."

"My hair too?"

"Aye, your hair too. Charley, my boy, you start filling pots from the tap. We'll have her scrubbed and polished in no time."

Charley scowled, but he took two cooking pots and went off down the hall to the tap, shared by the O'Dooleys with the Wongs and the Flanigans and the Goldsmiths. Nelly unhitched a washtub from a hook on the ceiling and set it on the floor next to the table.

"Couldn't we just rinse me off with a cloth?"

"Well, we could. But since you fit, you might as well sit down and have a real bath like the Queen of England over there in Buckingham Palace."

She emptied the first pot that Charley brought and passed it back to him.

"We'll hot up the next pot on the cooker. That'll make it easier to sit in."

Charley made two more trips before Nelly thanked him and shooed him out the door.

"You can take yourself out for a walk around the corner. We've got women's work to do."

"You don't mean I'm to be naked?" asked Josephine, as soon as he'd gone.

"Near enough," replied Nelly. "Now, don't worry yourself. A good bath never killed a person yet."

Josephine took off her dress and wrapped her arms about herself, not quite believing what Nelly expected of her.

"Oh, you can leave on your underthings if you're so edgy. They could do with a wash as well, I'm sure."

Josephine shut her eyes and lowered herself into the warm water. "Uck! I can feel the ridges on the bottom pressing into my legs." She didn't like to mention the bruises on her thighs.

Her chemise and pantalettes clung to her skin. She supposed it might feel this way to jump into a rain barrel after a summer rain. There was something unnatural about being so wet indoors.

Nelly dunked the soap bar and set to work, rubbing the lather all over, until Josephine squealed with laughter.

"Ah, she's ticklish, is she?" Nelly's fingers started to

wriggle and Josephine started to squirm, soon sending waves over the side of the tub to soak the floor.

"All right, we've got your hair to do yet. Let's not empty it all out." Without warning, Nelly dipped Josephine's whole head under the water and brought it back up before she had time to be scared.

"I went under!"

"Aye, that you did!"

Nelly set to soaping Josephine's curls.

"You've a lot of hair for a little person," she said, rinsing it clean with the water left in the pot.

"I snip it off sometimes, if it gets too wild. With my sewing scissors."

Laughing, Nelly helped her out of the tub and peeled off the sodden undergarments.

"I never saw a grown person laugh before," said Josephine. "I only know the mean variety with pinched-in lips."

"You've had a bad start, Missy, but I can make you a promise that there's laughter to be found in all but the darkest corners."

The bath ended with Nelly nearly as sopped as Josephine and one thin towel trying to do a job beyond its ability. Charley came home to find them still damp but well scoured, nibbling buns together like old ladies in an uptown tea shop.

Her bath was only the first of many novelties for Josephine that week.

After expressing his initial dismay at the cost of an entire wardrobe made to measure for Little Jo-Jo, Mr. Walters had become deeply interested in the process. He hired Eliot Jacobs, Custom Clothier, who promised a special rate due to the limited yardage involved. Mr. Jacobs had proven up to the challenge of creating miniature versions of gowns worn by great women of history: Cleopatra, Marie Antoinette of France, and Abraham Lincoln's fashionable wife, Mary, who was famous for her devotion to fancy dresses.

Josephine tolerated hours of fittings, standing on a table in Mr. Jacobs's workshop. From her unusually elevated vantage point, she could see every corner of the crowded studio. Looking like headless monsters, tailors' forms stood near the dusty windows, stuck with pins and pattern pieces. Bolts of fabrics were stacked on shelves up to the ceiling. Spools of ribbon, boxes brimming with buttons, and reels of thread littered every surface.

Josephine gazed down upon Mr. Jacobs's gleaming bald head and admired a master tailor at work. She turned, inch by inch, while Mr. Jacobs pinned here and fussed there.

"You're a patient little thing, I'll say that for you," praised Mr. Jacobs gruffly.

"I'm used to being told, is all," said Josephine shyly. "It's having someone sew for me I'm not used to. Instead of the other way around."

And along with being fitted for new clothes, she had two short lessons in how to wear them. How to walk, how to turn, and how to curtsy without falling on her nose.

Her feet, too, needed particular attention. The cobbler, a wizened Mr. Amos, was bent nearly to her own height from decades at his bench. He was delighted to create a whole series of ornate slippers, sized for a fairy.

"You're not the first tiny lady I've attended to!" he crowed.

"What do you mean?" asked Josephine, thinking she misunderstood him.

"It's over twenty years now, but Mr. P. T. Barnum himself hired me to make the wedding slippers for Miss Lavinia Bump Warren when she was married to General Tom Thumb!" He peered into Josephine's face. "You do know who I'm referring to? The most celebrated midgets ever known on this earth?"

"Yes!" said Josephine. "Of course I've heard of them!"

"General Tom Thumb died last year, may he rest in peace." Mr. Amos shook his head sadly.

"I guess I never thought about them being real people," said Josephine, "who wore shoes and hats and such. More like famous stories that somebody made up. You actually met Lavinia Warren?"

"I met her, I measured her feet, and I had the honor of crafting the slippers she wore to walk down the aisle of Grace Church on her wedding day!" Mr. Amos grinned at Josephine, displaying the three yellow teeth left in his mouth. "And I'll tell you the truth, my dearie. Your feet are smaller than hers."

Josephine suddenly had an idea.

"Mr. Amos?" she said, touching his arm.

"Eh?" Mr. Amos bent farther toward her so she could speak into his ear.

"I have a little money of my own, sir. Saved up from working before. What I really want is—" She hesitated. "I mean, all your fancy slippers are beautiful, sir, but what I want is a real pair of shoes. To just wear. And I'll pay."

The very next day, Josephine had her plain, brown leather high-lows with a buckle in front. Real shoes that really fit!

"Oh, Mr. Amos!"

"Well, they are pretty, if I do say so myself. I like a shoe that meets the ankle, but for a child the heel should be low to the ground. I'm happy you like them, my dearie."

And Josephine had bought them with two dollars of her own money! That made her think about having a new dress too. One that wasn't a costume, that she could wear every day instead of her raggedy kitchen dress. When consulted, Mr. Jacobs kindly agreed to create a simple frock in exchange for her remaining coins.

"You look as pretty as a picture postcard!" exclaimed Nelly fondly. "That green linen suits you. Brings out the color of your eyes."

Mr. Walters had also ordered six pairs of stockings, including striped ones, which Mr. Jacobs assured him were the very latest thing from France.

"Why, these would fit the hind legs of a cat!" Mr. Walters exclaimed, holding them up in amazement. And that gave him his next brilliant idea.

"Rosie has a big old dog, doesn't she, Nelly?"

"Aye, sir. His name is Barker. He's a retriever."

"Well, it's time he earned his keep. What do you say to riding a dog, Josephine? I shall order a saddle."

"Me? Ride a dog?"

Josephine thought briefly of the howling hounds that had chased her the night she fled from school.

"Will he be even-tempered, sir?"

Mr. Walters roared with laughter. "Every bit as pleasant as I am, my dear."

"I'm not sure that's a comfort," she murmured in reply.

Several days later, the wardrobe complete and her manners polished, Josephine sat in Mr. Walters's office. She listened in bemusement as he spoke at great length and great volume into a peculiar instrument on his desk called a telephone.

"Yes? Yes? Hello?" he shouted. "*New York Tribune*? This is R. J. Walters calling you. I want to notify your reporter of cultural affairs—that would be who? Who? Mr. Gideon Smyth? Thank you.

"Please notify Mr. Smyth of a reception being held at the New Amsterdam Hotel—Hello? Yes, to honor the sudden arrival of a new celebrity in our midst. All the way from Middle Europe. This is an occasion of great importance. He will want to be notified. Little Jo-Jo is the smallest human in the world—

"Tom Thumb? A giant by comparison! Come and see for yourself! On Friday evening at five o'clock. The New Amsterdam Hotel . . ."

Over and over, Mr. Walters made this invitation, to reporters and journalists at every newspaper within the range of his telephone.

When he finally replaced the handpiece and looked at Josephine, he bore the smile of a man proud of a long day's labor.

"Not everything you said was true," Josephine accused him. "What if they find out? What if I make a mistake?"

"Let me tell you something," said Mr. Walters, his voice humming with reassurance and warmth. "Not everything I told them needed to be true. It just had to be intriguing. In the world of entertainment, that is known as the ballyhoo—the talk that brings them in the door. Once they're inside, what they've been told will pale in the face of the real thing. And in this case, the real thing is you."

10

The Newspapers
Have Something to Say

NEW YORK TRIBUNE

Mr. R. J. Walters Discovers
WORLD'S
SMALLEST GIRL

WEDNESDAY, JUNE 4, 1884—Mr. Randolph James Walters, proprietor of the Museum of Earthly Astonishments located on the Bouwerie, and in Coney Island, today announced that he has discovered and employed what he claims to be the world's smallest woman currently on exhibition.

In a special viewing at the New Amsterdam Hotel in this City, hosted by the dapper Mr. Walters, the miniature native of Bavaria, known only as Little Jo-Jo, was introduced to the world.

This lovely lady is eighteen years old, weighs 19 pounds and measures 28-½ inches in height. She enjoys perfect health, her form is symmetrically developed, and her green eyes fairly sparkle with intelligence.

This City has not welcomed such a diminutive person

since the famous pair of General Tom Thumb and his lovely wife, Lavinia Bump Warren, were sponsored by P. T. Barnum, twenty years ago. R. J. Walters, while acknowledging the inspiring midgets who married in 1863, was quick to remind us that Little Jo-Jo is a full 3-1/2 inches smaller than Miss Warren.

Little Jo-Jo has dark, curling hair and slightly swarthy skin, leading Mr. Walters to suspect that she has some gypsy blood. This would explain her fiery temperament and her fondness for the tambourine. At times, her deportment about the hotel parlor was modest and ladylike, but she displayed moments of a spontaneous passion.

Mr. Walters reminded the audience that she has been living in foreign lands and made assurances that her adjustment to society would be swift and charming.

Little Jo-Jo's feet are only four inches long, but perfectly proportioned, and shod in beaded handmade slippers. Her dresses, by themselves, would be worthy of exhibition as each is a splendid recreation of an historical costume, elaborately embroidered and bejeweled. The dress and contents together are a magnificent show, already enjoying visits from some of the more prominent families in this City.

Little Jo-Jo will be on display at the Museum's summer location in Coney Island, New York, starting June 27th. She can be viewed on the platform in the Main Promenade from 10 o'clock A.M. to 8 o'clock P.M.

Notwithstanding this attraction alone is enough to fill the Museum to overflowing, also on view will be many of Mr. Walters' other novelties.

THE NEW YORK SUN

AMUSEMENTS

R. J. WALTERS'

MUSEUM OF EARTHLY ASTONISHMENTS

LITTLE JO-JO

PRINCESS OF THE LILLIPUTIANS
is the wonder of the City!

BE ONE OF THE FIRST
to be amazed at her

EXCEEDING DIMINUTIVE PROPORTIONS.
No larger than a good-sized doll. ONLY 28½ inches high
AND WEIGHS BUT 19 POUNDS.

THE SMALLEST GIRL
THE SMALLEST GIRL
THE SMALLEST GIRL

Despite many offers of
fabulous sums to display elsewhere,

HER PREMIERE APPEARANCE
HER PREMIERE APPEARANCE
HER PREMIERE APPEARANCE

is here at the Walters Hall in Coney Island.
For the trifling sum of 25 cents, you can

SEE HER EXQUISITE DRESSES,
SEE HER PRECIOUS JEWELS,
SEE HER DAINTY SHOES.

From 10 o'clock A.M. to 8 o'clock P.M. ☞ *Staged showings of special acts*
at 2 P.M. and 5 P.M. daily (15 cents extra).

Also on View: Other Living Curiosities **&**
Earthly Astonishments

*such as **The Alligator Man, The Bearded Lady,***
The Albino Boy, Exotic Snake Handler,
A Genuine Hippopotamus, and a great
variety of Tropical Birds from Distant Jungles.

Admission 25 cents   Children 15 cents

11

Josephine Arrives
at Coney Island

The train from the city took more than an hour, but because it was Josephine's first train ride ever, it wasn't long enough. Gazing up at the huffing steam engine, Josephine was amazed to see a machine so tremendous. Climbing aboard took every bit of bravery she'd saved up these past few days. And when it began to move—why, this iron monster seemed to be galloping as fast as any horse or faster!

Josephine stood on the bench, with Nelly and Charley sitting next to her, in a third-class compartment. She hung on to the windowsill, trying to see every block of the city flashing by.

"Don't you want to look out, Charley?"

"I can't really see anything past a few feet, Jo. It's my albino eyes. I don't take much pleasure from scenery."

"Oh, Charley, I didn't realize."

"Don't worry your wee self," said Nelly quickly. "He's used to it. Half-blind and skinny as a pencil, but still my handsome boy, eh, Charley?" She patted his knee.

Charley changed the subject. "This year is the first time we can take the train all the way there," he told Josephine. "We used to take the steamer ferry, but now, since the new bridge opened up last year, the train is the quickest way to go."

The Brooklyn Bridge spanned the river like a giant's castle drawbridge. It would never, could never, hold a railway train! As well as all those horses and carriages and carts wheeling along beside! Surely they would all hurtle through the cables holding it up and tumble into the water.

But the train crossed in safety and kept on chugging, spitting out smoke and soot, and joggling from side to side until Josephine's insides were churned like new butter.

Soon after the train crossed the bridge, the landscape changed. No longer city streets and people, now there were acres of coal yards and ash pits. Josephine turned away from the window.

"Are we allowed to move about?" she asked. "Can we explore the train?"

"Surely," said Charley. "There's other museum folk on board too. We're all moving out for the opening this weekend."

Nelly stayed where she was while Charley took Josephine in hand.

"I will be your Guide to the Fantastical," he announced, changing his voice to sound impressively like Mr. Walters. "I will show you things you have never seen before. . . ." The train rattled terribly as he led her down the passage.

"That's Rosie." Charley pointed though the window of the next-door compartment. A woman, who seemed oblivious to the motion, was knitting with gray wool.

"She's the Bearded Lady. She used to be the Fat Lady too, but she renounced buttered cake and has lost half her employ."

"Where's her beard?"

"She tucks it into that lacy shawl about her neck and chin. The beard is real, all right. Mr. Walters may be a honey-fuggler, trying on a trick from time to time, but Old Rosie is genuine. I tugged on those prickly whiskers when I was a kid, and she howled like a dog in a rat pit."

He opened the door to the compartment.

"Hey, Rosie! This is Josephine. She's the new featured exhibition."

"How do you do?" said Josephine. Rosie nodded without stopping her needles.

Lying asleep across Rosie's feet, his fur vibrating from the motion of the train, was an enormous dog, the color of butterscotch candy.

"That's Barker," said Charley. "That's the beast you're supposed to go gallivanting about on."

"Him?" Josephine stared. His body covered most of the floor between benches. His tail alone seemed at least half her height. How big would he be standing up?

"Hey, Barker!" called Charley. The dog opened one eye and closed it again with a slight snore. Rosie shifted her knitting needles to one hand and leaned down to give him a pat.

"He's a good boy," she said, clucking softly. "He's been with me these eleven years."

"I don't think you have a lot to worry about, Jo," Charley sniggered. "He doesn't seem to be much of a stallion."

Josephine eyed Barker's tremendous paws, folded neatly over his nose.

"He could knock me flat with one swat!" she said.

"Well, then," answered Charley, with sparkling eyes, "you'd best make friends with him."

"How do I do that?"

"He likes his ears tugged on," advised Rosie. "Just so." She demonstrated. Josephine didn't think she'd dare.

"Or," said Charley, "you could let him tug on yours!"

They returned to the corridor just as the train lurched, tipping Josephine onto her backside with a thump. Charley scooped her up and held her for a moment while the train hammered on.

"Hey!" Josephine wriggled, as her cheeks flared with warmth. "I'm not a baby."

"Don't be wrathy! I was only saving your life."

Charley set her down and turned away. Josephine bent over, pretending to adjust her stocking, while she cooled down. It had been a shock to find herself in Charley's arms, but he seemed to think nothing of it. He was merely continuing the tour. He poked his neck into another compartment, pushing Josephine in front.

"This is Eddie."

Eddie looked up from reading and smiled with friendly curiosity.

"Excuse us, Eddie. This here is Josephine. She's the new one Mr. Walters used to fill up his amusements advertisement."

"Ah, yes! Little Jo-Jo. It's an honor to meet you." Eddie bowed awkwardly from his sitting position, and blinked soft, brown eyes before returning to his book.

Josephine clutched Charley's jacket tail as they held on in the corridor.

"He seems a comely enough gentleman." She tried to keep her voice low and yet still be heard above the racket of the wheels. "What does Mr. Walters use him for?"

"Oh, his face is fine and likely," said Charley, "but underneath his clothing, his skin is like a prehistoric reptile."

"He's the Alligator Man?"

"He's got a horrible ailment," Charley told her with relish. "A rare condition that makes his skin look scaly and cracked like the bark of an old tree. It's so plug-ugly you could cry."

Josephine looked back over her shoulder. That gentle, pleasant face was sitting atop a lizardly body? She found that she, too, could be astonished.

"Hey! Filipe! I didn't see you at the station!" Charley punched the arm of an older boy, who tapped him back with a grin.

"Where are the snakes?" asked Charley.

"Snakes?" asked Josephine.

"They're not allowed on the train," answered Filipe. His accent was different from that of Nelly and Charley. "They will ride tomorrow on the roof of Mr. Walters's carriage."

Filipe's dashing yellow cap barely contained his thatch of black hair. His skin was the color of coffee with milk poured into it. Next to him, Charley looked as white as a marble floor.

"Marco and Polo are pythons," explained Charley.

"Uck," said Josephine.

"Those snakes are so big they'd eat you for supper, Jo."

Filipe eyed her, considering. "It's true, I think. You are not so big as a one-year pig. This would make a good supper."

He and Charley punched each other again, laughing out loud with their mouths wide open.

Josephine bit the inside of her lip. She felt the train shaking under her, matching the quivers of anger inside. Charley should know better than to tease about her size. How would he feel if she called him—what could she call him that would hurt? How about Paste Face? Or Ghost Boy?

"Never mind the boys, they get silly and cut shines." Nelly was suddenly beside her. "Look here, we've arrived. We'll see the ocean!"

Josephine was lifted from the train like a picnic basket and set on the platform of the Coney Island station.

She felt the ocean in the air almost like a slap, before she even saw it.

Oh, the ocean!

No one had prepared her for the ocean. She knew it was there, of course; there were oceans in books about sailing ships, and it was a spreading blue background on the map in the Academy's geography classroom.

But no one had said the word "ocean" in an ecstatic whisper with shining eyes and clasped hands and body tilted as if feeling the salty wind.

And then she saw it for herself! A huge, glittering carpet, shifting and rolling under the summer sun, like acres of spangled silk! This ocean was here all the time? She could come every day to smell the fresh, tangy air. To hear the perpetual rumble and crash of the foaming waves. To watch the sparkle on the water, like countless floating jewels.

The sting of Charley's teasing faded away. The whole week of being measured for fancy clothes and smiling at newspapermen disappeared.

Josephine couldn't believe her luck. She had an ocean!

12
IN WHICH Little Jo-Jo
Makes Her First Appearance

Josephine's first day of employ at the Museum of Earthly Astonishments in Coney Island was one she would remember for all of her life.

Nelly fed her bites of toasted bread while she dressed, because she had no stomach for the oatmeal porridge that Charley devoured each morning. During her regular exhibition hours, Mr. Walters had decreed that Josephine wear a dress of rose-colored satin with a purple petticoat and lavender stockings. If she were to fall down and give a view of her underpinnings, she'd look like a garden in full bloom!

Charley wore his customary work uniform of a black suit with a pink cravat, which made his eyes glitter like blushing crystals.

"You look about to be married, Charley O'Dooley!" said Josephine.

"Oooeee! You're almighty comely yourself when you're slicked up, Jo!" And when she looked in the glass propped against the wall, she had to agree. Her hair was pinned up into a real lady's chignon, adding several years to her face. Nelly had insisted that a few curls escaping at the back were the height of fashion.

Nelly, who gave up her job at the Half-Dollar Saloon

during the summer months, would be in charge of the admissions booth at the museum. That way she could fill in as stage mother when required to help Josephine change her costumes.

On the outside walls of Walters Hall were hung enormous, painted banners, shouting to the world of the marvels that dwelt within.

EDUARDO, THE ALLIGATOR MAN, HALF HUMAN, HALF REPTILE!

and then a picture of Eddie's scaly body beneath his grimacing face.

CHARLES, THE ALBINO BOY! DARE TO MEET A WALKING GHOST!

Charley, colored with the whitest pigment in the paint box, leered out at the customers with demonic eyes.

LITTLE JO-JO! THE WORLD'S SMALLEST GIRL!

The portrait of Josephine showed her standing on an upturned teacup next to a flowerpot, with daisies towering over her.

The Main Promenade of Walters Hall sounded grander than it could ever be. Really, it was a long, narrow room with low ceilings, painted a yellow that was meant to say "carnival" but said instead "no sunlight here." Instead of brightening the hall, winking gas flames only added to the gloom.

Except during showtimes, the Astonishments were to stand at intervals along the hallway, still as stones on the beach, and let folks stare to their hearts' content—or at least till they were pushed along by the crowd behind.

All the Strange Humans were staged indoors. The Genuine Hippopotamus and a motley flock of parrots were kept in a pen through an alley to the rear.

According to Charley, the hippopotamus had joined the company last summer. In the beginning, it was Mr. Walters's great prize, being the only such creature to be exhibited anywhere in the state, as far as he knew.

But Potty was a great, grouchy thing, with breath that could knock down a tree. And arranging for a permanent mud puddle had proved to be a trial.

"Mr. Walters says he's looking to find a mate for our Potty," confided Charley. "The old stinker ought to liven up some having a lady to share his muck with. And a baby hippo would be worth its own weight in admission fees."

It was in the alley alongside Potty's pen where Josephine had learned to ride upon Barker's back. Not wanting to admit to her fluttering stomach, she had asked that no one watch except the dog's mistress, Rosie.

Rosie's concern seemed more for Barker than for Josephine, but the Bearded Lady had been gentle enough when lifting her onto the saddle.

Josephine sat astride, her feet just level with Barker's golden underbelly. There was a rein, but only for the look of it. Josephine's hands held fistfuls of tawny fur at Barker's neck, which she tried not to yank while the patient dog padded back and forth, serenaded by bleating parrots.

"Ah, Jo-Jo," confessed Rosie, "I'd trade in my best corset for a few minutes in your place right now. I always knew my Barker was a good boy, but with you setting there on top, he looks right royal."

"I do feel . . ." Josephine found herself whispering. "He makes me feel as a princess might, the way he puts his paws down so careful. Not shaking me off, but trying to help me sit tall."

When Mr. Walters had been summoned to watch a demonstration, he bowed low and held out his hand to help Josephine dismount.

"A fine addition!" he applauded. "Another astonishing first for my Museum!"

Indoors, apart from the living exhibitions, there were several glass cases displaying what Mr. Walters claimed to be an "Impressive Selection of Collected Curiosities."

Charley had to lift Josephine up so that she could see. There was a dried ear from an African elephant next to a glass bottle holding twelve black beetles found in the stomach of a baby in Pennsylvania.

"Uck!" laughed Josephine. "She must have been a crabby little thing."

"What I'd like to know," said Charley, "was whether the baby died because she had the bugs in her belly? Or whether she spat them out, one by one, and lived to be a wrinkled old lady."

"With a daily craving for crawly bugs!" added Josephine. "And what about that?" she asked, pointing. "How does anyone know that crackedy old stick came from George Washington's chopped-down cherry tree?"

"Because Mr. Walters tells them so! Along with the rest of his flummery."

On an ebony pedestal, there was a mounted cat with only one leg.

"It was supposedly born that way," said Charley, in a vicious whisper. "But I swear that Mr. Walters cut off the other three legs."

"That's just plain horrible," said Josephine. "And so is that." She stared at the tattooed hand of a Maori chieftain preserved in brine.

There was a hat that once belonged to former President Ulysses S. Grant and the handcuffs that had escorted the famous bank robber Paddy Parker to prison.

" 'A feather from the pillow of Queen Victoria herself'?" Josephine laughed so hard that Charley had to put her down.

"You have to believe, once you're in here," explained Charley. "You'd feel an almighty fool if you paid twenty-

five cents and thought the feather came from the goose
around the corner!"

Despite his promise to Josephine that he would
exhibit her beyond the reach of curious fingers, Mr.
Walters had not seemed inclined to spend money on a
special platform. But clever Nelly had convinced him.

"Surely the customers will think she's something more
than humdrum if you put her up there like a wee
princess. You've paid so many dollars on her clothes and
shoes, it'd be a shame not to show her off to the best
advantage."

"Hmmm." Mr. Walters chewed on his whiskers.
"Maybe you've got something there, Nelly O'Dooley."
He agreed reluctantly. "If you weren't a woman, you'd
make a fine businessman."

The platform stood five feet off the floor, with a
wooden ladder at one end for Josephine to get up and
down. Mr. Walters had decorated it using furniture sam-
ples made smaller for the convenience of traveling sales-
men.

"Just as you requested, my dear," said Mr. Walters to
Josephine, early on the first morning. "Go on up and try
it out."

Josephine hitched up her swirling satin skirt and
climbed the tiny ladder with the ease of a sailor. She
stroked the doll's flowered tea set, laid out on the little
table. "I've never had things my own size! Oh, Mr.
Walters! Thank you!"

Mr. Walters watched her sit on the chair, with his eyebrows dipped in a frown.

"It's not right," he declared finally. "It's the wrong approach entirely."

Josephine's heart sank. Mr. Walters looked around for one of the workmen, who was dabbing paint over the winter's stains and blisters.

"Ippy. Take these little things and put them in storage until that salesman comes through this way again. I'll get my money back. And I need a big chair instead. A very big chair. Big enough for *me* to sink into. Do you understand? Now!"

Ippy's left eye twitched as he slunk off with a hopeless curve to his shoulders. But within an hour, he returned, balancing an enormous armchair on a wagon. It took three men and a symphony of grunting to get it atop the platform, but they managed.

Josephine's chair was now big enough to swallow her, which was just the effect that Mr. Walters wanted to emphasize. She was, after all, the world's smallest girl.

At the warning bell, the Astonishments took their places along the main promenade, with Josephine overseeing it all from her lofty perch.

When the doors swung open, the morning sunshine spilled only a few feet into the mysterious interior of Walters Hall. Folks were lined up outside, maybe fifty or more. Mr. Walters was rubbing his hands in anticipation.

"The petticoats are paid for already!" he gloated. His advertisement in the newspapers had made Little Jo-Jo the main attraction of opening day.

A noisy herd of sweating patrons pushed into the gallery. Their feet thumped on the wooden floor as they rushed past the exhibits by the entrance, seeking Little Jo-Jo in the place of honor on the back wall.

A secret ripple of pleasure made her shiver as she saw the crowd before her. This might be fun! She sat in the giant chair and adjusted her tiny shoe. They sighed. She walked to the edge of the platform and smirked down at them. They fluttered in awe. Whatever she did was marvelous!

At two o'clock, for the Show of Curiosities (costing an extra fifteen cents above the admission price), there was not an empty seat in the tent. Josephine stood backstage, aware suddenly that her chest had tightened, making breathing difficult. Her giddy excitement combined with the smell of moldy canvas made her feel quite sick. Her hands felt cold but were damp with sweat.

She heard Mr. Walters's ballyhoo and then the drumroll, announcing her first appearance. She was dressed as Cleopatra, in a black wig and silk shift spun with gold thread. She walked onstage and heard the audience gasp. Had she made a mistake and entered at the wrong time? No, now they were applauding! For her!

By the time she entered for the finale, wearing a riding habit astride dear Barker's back, the audience was wild with excitement. Josephine was the new star of Coney Island!

13
IN WHICH Josephine Gets a Letter

MacLaren Academy
June 27, 1884

Dear Josephine,
I was worried and afraid after you went away, not
knowing where you went. My sister, Margaret, wrote
me you never came, then we saw the newspaper, a story
about Little Jo-Jo and I knew it was you, I was glad
for you to be getting famous instead of beaten, Miss
MacLaren went quite red when she saw the article,
with purple veins on her nose. Catherine showed her the
newspaper, Nancy bought it with a penny stole from
the chapel box, she saw the story first, I was so very glad
to know you are safe.

> *God Bless, your friend,*
> *Emmy*

P.S. Cook has a new girl, Sylvester's cousin, Pauline,
she's got warts.

14

Charley and Josephine
Have a Little Holiday

The first time Josephine met Mrs. Hilda
Viemeister, she was crushed against the
woman's bosom in a suffocating embrace.

"Precious chick," clucked Hilda, replacing Josephine
on the floor, dizzy and bemused.

Mrs. Hilda Viemeister had the fortune, be it good or
bad, to have inherited two row houses side by side, one
from her dead brother and the other from her dead husband. They had been killed, side by side, in front of a
saloon, by a runaway horse bus. Upon their deaths, Mrs.
Viemeister had begun immediately to take in boarders,
to pay for the coal and the food on her table.

Nelly and Charley had stayed at her lodgings every
summer that the museum had been open at Coney
Island. Eddie was also boarding there this year. Unlike
most others in her business, Hilda Viemeister had a
fondness for circus folk. She didn't mind that they wandered in and out of her life, she didn't notice that they
often looked peculiar. She did mind if they left a mess
or if they expected more from her than clean linens once
a month and a hot supper.

For Josephine, Hilda's house became the home that
she shared with her new family. Day after day, Josephine

climbed the ladder to her platform with a lifting heart, ready to try new tricks to enchant her audience. And night after night, she walked home with Nelly and Charley, guessing which kind of stew Hilda would serve for supper.

Each morning, Hilda sent them off with a pat and a piece of bread and butter, always using the same words, "Don't work too hard, my little chickies. Keep your feathers fluffy!"

"Hey, you up there!" Charley stood below Josephine's platform and tugged on her skirt. "Get down! We've got two hours' liberty."

Josephine ignored groans of disappointment from the line of ogling customers. She skipped down the ladder and past the onlookers with a grin.

"See how small I am!" she shouted gaily, waving at them. To Charley, she whispered, "What are we doing?"

"You're daft," said Charley. "And what we're doing is, Mr. Walters has gone into the city, so we can all take a turn having a little holiday. Unless I take you to the loony bin instead. Come on. No lollygagging!"

Josephine was pulling the pins from her chignon and finger combing her curls within seconds.

"Can we go to the beach, Charley, please? We've been here days and days and only seen the inside of this smelly hall. I haven't even touched the sand yet, or the ocean. Please?"

"Sure, we're going to the beach. Where else to keep your feathers fluffy?"

Charley waited by the dressing room door while she changed into her dress. Her beautiful, very own, green linen dress.

"You can even go swimming, if you like. They rent swimming costumes at the bath house on the sand."

"I don't want to go actually into the water. There's too much of it. A person going in there might disappear in a wink. I just want to look at it. Besides, I'm, I'm—" She decided to make it funny. "Although my form is symmetrically developed, my proportions are diminutive."

Charley smiled down at her.

"Maybe they have baby sizes."

She pretended to kick him.

"Let's go."

The moment they were outside, Charley opened an umbrella that Josephine had not noticed he carried.

"Who's the loony now?" she asked. "It's not raining."

"The sun is poison to someone like me," said Charley. "So I have to be fashionable and carry a parasol."

He held the umbrella high in his left hand. He swept his right hand across the scene before them. It was a world alive with summer pleasures. The front door of Walters Hall opened directly onto the esplanade and faced the beach.

Hundreds of parasols were on parade, in dozens of colors. Ladies were dressed like so many sorbets and men were in summer suits and straw hats. Somewhere there was music playing, a violin and an accordion maybe. The air was bringing wafts of salt and fish and burnt sugar. Hawkers called attention to fruit, sweets and shaved ice, peanuts, potatoes, and chowder.

"Welcome to Coney Island, Jo! What do you want to eat first? Sweet corn? A hot potato? Oysters?"

"What's oysters?"

"You've never had oysters? Come on! Over here, see? The boys are shucking oysters. An oyster is a sort of a fishy thing that comes in a shell from the sea, but it doesn't swim, it just sits there."

"They look horrible! They're not fish at all! They look like bits of innards from a dead bird. Eeeew!"

Josephine couldn't believe her eyes. Charley had given the boy a penny. He beamed while his plateful of oysters was shucked, and slipped the first one into his mouth with a wink.

"Not even cooked?" Josephine felt her throat swell in disgust. She wouldn't look while he finished them off.

They wandered on.

"Come this way, ladies. Step along here, gentlemen!"

"Hey! Listen! I recognize that voice!" Charley peered around him, trying to find its source.

A man wearing a crimson vest over his shirt strutted back and forth. He cracked his knuckles and then continued his chanting song.

"I have the fantastic ability to guess your weight without the assistance of a scale or device of any kind. Who will be the first to test my skills?"

"I knew it!" said Charley. "Watch that fellow closely.

Tell me what he does next. He's a scalawag in disguise."

"He's just talking," said Josephine.

"Is there a gent nearby with a lot of pockets?"

"Yes, and he's a bit plump. He's stepping up now to the first fellow."

"Best actor on the beach," murmured Charley. "Keep watching."

"You don't mind me seeing what's clothes and what isn't, do you sir?" The crimson-vested fellow kept up his cheerful chatter while he patted the volunteer on the shoulders and the back and the sides.

"That tummy I can guess without touching!" he announced, drawing a laugh from the gathering crowd.

"This man!" he went one. "This man, who does not restrain his appetite . . . This man weighs two hundred and seventeen pound!"

The plump man's mouth fell open. "He's got it right! I was at the doctor only yesterday, and the scales said two hundred and seventeen if they said an ounce!"

"How did he do that?" Josephine was amazed.

The two men shook hands and the plump one handed over a nickel. "Well done! This is a clever fellow!" He declared to all who listened.

"Who's next?" asked the weight guesser. "Don't be shy! I can whisper, if you don't want the tonnage known generally . . ."

"There's another fellow now," said Josephine. "Not quite so fat, wearing a smart, new bowler hat."

"You don't mind me seeing what's clothes and what isn't, do you sir?" The routine had begun again.

The new customer wore a genial smirk while he was being patted and assessed. This time, however, the guess was off by twenty-two pounds, and the crowd jeered its disappointment.

"Are you watching?" said Charley. "Did you see anything?"

Josephine had noticed nothing that might have Charley dancing about on his toes like this. The bystanders were dispersing, on to more captivating games.

"Keep watching the man with the pockets, Jo. He's the secret."

The man weighing two hundred and seventeen pounds, Josephine reported, had paused on the beach, just a few yards away. The weight-guesser sidled close to him.

"He's passed him something that sent off a twinkle in the sun!" announced Josephine. "Something gold!"

"I told you!" crowed Charley, as if he himself had done the nimble deed. "That watch belonged to the Bowler Hat only moments ago!"

"How did you know?" asked Josephine, in amazement. "Without even seeing!"

"These two gents are partners and have worked the avenue every summer I can remember. They're very good. They only get arrested once or twice a year. And

coppers'll take spondulicks quick as any man. So they're
back the next day."

"Spondulicks? Charley, where do you come up with
these words?"

"Just means cash money, but it sounds better, doesn't it?"

"I don't know what you're so chirk for, Charley.
You'll be picking pockets yourself next. Now, come on,
I'm taking off my high-lows. I want to touch the ocean
with my plain bare feet!"

She unbuckled her boots and peeled off her stockings.
She shoved them into Charley's pockets and set out
across the beach, curling her toes and squealing at the
heat of the sand on her soles.

All around her, men and women alike were wearing
dark, woolen bathing costumes. The women's were
short dresses, with flared skirts and puffed sleeves and
sometimes sailor collars. Most of them wore black stockings too, so that every inch was covered, except for
freckled arms. The men revealed their hairy legs, poking
out from tight black suits.

"They look like camisoles stitched onto drawers.
Aren't they silly!"

Josephine was fascinated by the multitude of knees.
"Knees are really very ugly when seen in a large crop
like this," she said to Charley with a giggle.

The ocean was kicking up waves today, green and
frothy, dragging pebbles with each roll. Josephine let
only her toes get wet, unnerved by the churning pull
under her feet. Children ran toward the water and then

tumbled back, shrieking, as the foam leapt at them. Grown-ups were shrieking too, trying to tiptoe into the surf and getting knocked sideways. A long line of laughing people grasped the swimming rope, which was tethered between a pole on the beach and another pole twenty yards into the water.

"Can you swim, Charley?"

"No. It wouldn't be good for my skin."

"Well, I mean to learn, maybe, one day."

"Someone your size could probably float without trying. I'll bet Filipe knows how. You could ask him."

A pair of boys holding shovels and tin buckets stopped right in front of Josephine and stared. Then they looked up at Charley, who grimaced with a monstrous face, swivelling his pink eyes.

"Mama!" One of them howled, and they both ran.

"We'd best be off," said Charley. "Mr. Walters doesn't like us being looked at without him getting the pennies in his pocket." Reluctantly Josephine turned away from the ocean and headed back toward the esplanade.

"That sounds like something my pa might say," said Josephine. "He was a schemer, too, though he could learn a few tricks from Mr. Walters."

"You never said about your pa," said Charley, "or your mum either. I thought they might be dead."

"They might be," said Josephine. "But I wouldn't know it."

Charley was waiting for more, she could tell. How to explain?

"Your mother loves you, Charley. The way she pesters you and rubs your hair, I can see it. She doesn't care you're the color of paste."

"You're telling me your mum didn't love you? Because you're wee?"

"I think she might have loved me when I was a baby. She must have." Josephine was pretty certain about that, though she couldn't remember.

"But when I didn't grow . . . folks told her I was cursed. They left things beside our door, amulets and little crosses." Josephine hadn't thought about this in a long time. Her throat felt clogged. "I found a doll one time with no legs. I thought it was a present and I tried to fix her. That convinced the neighbors I was evil and a sign from the devil. My mother got to be afraid of me. My pa was practical; he thought I could be worth something. But my ma was afraid more than anything. She didn't want me to be hers anymore."

"Nelly says my dad took one look at me and ran out the door," said Charley quietly, twirling the umbrella slowly above his head, making the shadow spin on the sand. "She never saw him again."

"I wish—" said Josephine. "Can I tell you? I wish that people could grow up before they had to have a family. So they would know what sort of folk they wanted to be family with. Then we could choose for ourselves."

"I suppose that's what your mum was doing," said Charley.

"You mean choosing not to have me anymore?"

Charley nodded, his eyes shifting away.

"I never thought of that," said Josephine.

"Or maybe she just meant to free you up, to find the right family for you." Charley liked that idea better. "And see? You found Nelly and me."

"It took an awful long time. And you and Filipe had better stop teasing me, Charley O'Dooley, or I'll keep looking!"

"What do you think brothers do, Jo? We tease. And I'm thinking I need more practice. . . ."

15
IN WHICH Josephine Receives Another Letter

MacLaren Academy
July 8, 1884

Dear Josephine,
I keep wondering if you have ever got my letter?
Perhaps you could write back to me to tell me that all is
well? I keep wondering what it might be like to live in
the circus which I imagine is something like where you
are. Nancy and Anne went to Mr. PT Barnum's circus
with Nancy's father, they said there was a wild tiger and
the tamer had diamonds on his shirt, also a lady who
had bare legs and hung upside down from a trapeze.

*School is just as dreary and so hot I can hardly stay
awake during sums, I wish you were here to be my
friend.*

God Bless, your friend,
Emmy

16
IN WHICH Charley and Josephine Go for a Ride

The sun's been shining every day like it had a prize to win." Charley was complaining again and kicking at Josephine's ladder. When he stood beside her platform and she lay on her tummy, Josephine could look straight into his face. They were waiting for the opening bell to ring, for the spectators to pour into the dark hall like ants into molasses.

"Your mood is black enough to darken the sky, Charley. Maybe you could just scowl into the daylight and scare it away."

"It's fine for you to make fun, Jo. You go brown like a sailor out there. I blister up like old paint."

"It's not as though I have a chance to sniff the air myself, Charley! We're both stuck in this cave from the morning bell till night!"

The toe of Charley's boot was scuffed bare from kicking. Josephine had never seen him in such a mood.

"How about—?" She tried to think. What might cheer him up? "How about, let's not go straight back to the boarding house after closing. It'll be evening then, no sun to worry about. You can show me the sights."

"*We're* the sights," grumbled Charley. "But I suppose I could, if it'll make you happy."

Eight o'clock found them strolling away from the museum in high spirits.

"We'll turn left on Surf Avenue," said Charley. "Opposite to if we were going home."

Tonight they were tourists. The street was abuzz with the evening trade. Beachgoers paused on their way to the train, hungry to shop from carts brimming with oysters, clams, corn, chowder, pork pies, and ham sandwiches. Other folk were just arriving, anticipating a night of dancing or card-playing.

Even at Josephine's level, there was plenty to look at. She was an expert on ladies' shoes and carriage wheels and the array of wonders to be found in the gutter of any city block. So when Charley tapped her head, she was amazed to find herself staring up at an enormous elephant made of tin. Josephine was not even as big as one of its painted toenails.

"What's that?"

"That's Lucy. It's a hotel inside. With a dance floor and a store and thirty-four rooms for sleeping in."

"Can we look?"

Charley shook his head. "Nelly would tan my hide if I took you there. They pretend you could stay there with a family, but really it's for gamblers and drinkers and ladies who sell their affections." He glanced at her to see if she understood. He was certainly cheered to be in the role of a tour guide.

"Nothing you like better," said Josephine, "than to know more than every other body."

Charley smiled at her, resting his fingertips lightly on her curls as he usually did when they walked together these days. He turned her gently around, and they headed back along Surf Avenue.

"I've noticed something about you, Jo."

"And that would be?"

"I've noticed that your teasing skills are improving. You are almost worthy of being a sister."

"Hah!" scoffed Josephine. "And who chose you to be the judge of that?"

He gave her a poke and she poked him back. They wandered along for a bit, noticing how the music got louder as the sky darkened and the smell of beer grew stronger.

"Did you ever eat in a restaurant, Charley?"

"Oh sure, lots of times. Well, twice. And maybe more that I'm not recalling."

"How could you not remember eating your supper in a restaurant?"

"Nelly took me to Feltman's for my birthday last year.

It's in September, just before we move back to the city."

"What's Feltman's?"

"See, over there: Feltman's German Beer Garden." He pointed to a large establishment with a street band playing outside its doors. The musician tooting on the cornet was wearing leather pants that stopped above the knees.

"Did you drink beer?"

"We ate the specialty of the house. Sausages served inside a roll instead of on a plate."

"Doesn't it slip about?"

"No, the bread grabs it like a mitten. But Filipe says that Feltman's sausages are made of dog meat, that's why they're called hot dogs."

"Eeeew, Charley, don't tell me that! Think of Barker ground up and turned into sausages!"

"Hey!" whooped Charley suddenly, "I've got an idea! Come on, Jo! I'll wager you've never ridden on a bicycle!"

Before Josephine could utter a word, Charley had left her standing alone while he galloped away toward a shed with a painted sign overhead that shouted:

WOOD'S BICYCLES 10¢

Josephine raced after him, dodging a wagon loaded with beer barrels and arriving in time to see the bicycle boy staring at Charley with deep suspicion.

"Never seen a ghost before, boy?" Charley was saying.

"No, sir."

"Well, take a good look." Charley lifted his tinted spectacles and bugged out his flaming eyes. The boy stepped back in alarm.

"I'll be needing a bicycle for two cents instead of ten," said Charley, "or I'll be haunting you till the day you're a ghost yourself."

"Charley!"

"Shush!"

The boy seemed grateful to take two pennies and disappear into the shed. One minute later, Charley was astride a rusty black bicycle, wearing a grin as wide as his face would stretch.

"Climb aboard!" he said.

"You've lost what little brains you ever had, Charley O'Dooley! You want me to get aboard that contraption? Where am I supposed to sit?" Josephine eyed the wheels, higher than her own head.

"Oh, she's a fancy lady now, is she? Wants a gilded carriage wherever she goes!"

Charley laughed as he leaned over, balancing the bicycle between his legs. He put his hands firmly under Josephine's arms and swung her up, dress aflutter, to the handlebars, where he plunked her down with not a spot of respect. She clung to the bars for her very life, which set Charley to laughing even harder.

"Can you see well enough to drive this thing, Charley? I don't want to crash into a buggy or a-aaAAAH!"

Charley had started to pedal and the bicycle wobbled

forward, finding every bump in the road and picking up speed. Josephine clamped her lips to stop herself from screaming but forced her eyes open. They rattled past vendors and shoppers alike, at a pace that made Josephine's head spin. And perhaps because Charley couldn't see the numerous wagons and horses clogging the road, he kept swerving at the last moment before impact.

"This is rip-roaring!" hooted Charley. "Isn't it?"

"Oh wait, Charley! Wait, stop! No, no, keep going! Look out! Ow!"

The bicycle lurched to a stop, inches away from a small group of people at a stall that sold lemonade.

Josephine was nearly flung off, but for her quick-gripping hands and Charley's left arm snaking around her neck at the last moment.

"Whoa!"

The roughness of the stop, however, along with Josephine's croak of terrified laughter and Charley's yelp of joy made the cluster of lemonade buyers turn to stare.

And who should be standing there but Nancy and Charlotte from the MacLaren Academy. Charlotte's eyes nearly popped right out of her head, they opened so wide. Nancy clapped her hand to her mouth and spilled her lemonade all down the front of her pinafore.

"Hello, girls!" Charley greeted them cheerfully, clearly hoping for the usual horrified reaction to his appearance.

A man who must be Nancy's father pulled out his pocket handkerchief. He scolded Charley while dabbing awkwardly at his daughter's bodice.

"You foolish boy! Are you blind?"

"Near enough," smirked Charley.

"How dare you careen down a populated street as if you were on a racetrack? You're a danger to well-mannered citizens!"

Josephine couldn't help but agree. Her palms were rubbed raw from hanging on so tightly. But Charley's tongue-lashing could wait. Nancy and Charlotte needed seeing to first.

They were gawping at her in true shock. Charlotte's face, so often pink, was all the way scarlet. Nancy, recovering more quickly, pointed at Josephine with a jabbing finger.

"You!" she bellowed. "You!"

Her father looked up in surprise, and then peered at Josephine more closely.

"Aren't you the little servant person from the school?" he inquired, looking at his daughter for confirmation.

Oh, but she wasn't their servant anymore! She could do whatever she pleased.

"You'll have to excuse us," she said, producing a British accent out of thin air. "We have an engagement and mustn't be late. Please drive on, Charles!"

And Charley obliged at once, wheeling the bicycle around them and pushing off to continue their ride, acting as though nothing in the world could stop them.

17
IN WHICH Emmy Writes Again

MacLaren Academy
August 3, 1884

Dear Josephine,

I know you work very long hours in your new situation, so I'm not minding that you haven't written to me yet, perhaps you did not receive my other letters?

I know that you are Little Jo-Jo now, because Nancy and Charlotte were in such a twitter when they came back on Sunday. Nancy's father takes her anywhere that features dancing girls, Nancy says he has a soft heart for dancing girls. (I'm sure I wouldn't say such a thing about my father unless I wanted a scolding and no supper.) He wouldn't pay for them to go into the Museum of Earthly Astonishments to see "freaks and ruffians" (his words) (also theirs, but not mine), so they were very lucky to see you. Miss MacLaren said it was a disgrace that they went to Coney Island, but she put on her spectacles and asked a hundred questions. They didn't tell me, I heard them telling Harriet, they said you were alone with a boy, but I don't believe them.

God Bless, your friend,
Emmy

18
Josephine's Past
Collides with Her Present

A scarlet curtain, smelling of months in a trunk, separated the stage part of the tent from the audience. Hidden from Josephine by the heavy drape, the hot, rustling patrons filled the tent to its seams.

As the weeks had gone by, Josephine had begun the habit of wrapping herself in the soft, grimy folds of velvet while she waited for her cue to appear for the special stage performance. She liked the rumbling words of Mr. Walter's ballyhoo. She could forget his sharp edges when she listened to the warm reverberation of his voice.

"Hurry! Hurry! Hurry! Squeeze in while you can!

"My Lucky Ladies, My Clever Gentlemen! You have come to Walters Hall to be Mesmerized by Curiosities of Nature, Unparalleled Elsewhere! I have devoted many years of Distant Travel and Exploration to uncover such Rare Marvels as those you will see here today."

Josephine peeked out at the swarm of expectant faces and saw something so familiar, and yet so out of place, that it took her a moment to realize what was before her.

"Perhaps," continued Mr. Walters, stroking his handsome moustache, "perhaps you expect to be Alarmed or Frightened or Horrified. That's as it should be, Ladies! Even your husbands will be a little of all these things."

Right at the front, just below the edge of the stage, was a row of identical straw hats. Each had a royal blue ribbon and a badge on the front. Josephine couldn't read the gold letters from where she was, but, having stitched every badge in place herself, she knew what they said:

MacLaren Academy
Fine School for Fine Girls

"But!" Mr. Walters's voice now dropped to a confidential whisper. "It is my dearest hope that you will go home with a shudder of contentment. That you will witness the Amazing and be satisfied that you are Plain and Ordinary, of no Interest to Anybody. Be content that you are not an Earthly Astonishment!"

Josephine clutched the curtain, feeling as though a hundred horses were galloping through her skull. She squeezed her eyes shut, as if that would make the audience disappear. But when she looked again, she could identify the faces tipped up to watch Mr. Walters, mouths agape with fascination.

Catherine's hat was crooked, as usual. Harriet's spectacles were smeared, and Anne's teeth poked out like those of a beaver. Nancy's lips were rimmed with chocolate, Charlotte's face was as blotched as ever, and Felicia's ringlets were limp in the heat.

And Emmy, dear Emmy, standing plump and awkward in their midst, looked suddenly to Josephine like the dearest friend she'd ever known. As a group, however, the Fine Girls of MacLaren Academy looked like hungry frogs, greeting a cloud of gnats descending on a pond.

She should have known that meeting Nancy and Charlotte was a bad omen, not a prank. If only she'd paid better attention to Emmy's letter! She'd almost sent a warning!

Josephine felt a nudge from behind.

"Go on! It's you! He's done your bit twice!" It was Charley, poking her.

Josephine realized that the thundering in her head was actually the drumroll announcing her arrival onstage. She untwisted the curtain and tumbled forward across the boards, tripping on the hem of her Mary Lincoln ball gown and only just managing to stay upright.

"Ladies and Gentlemen! Little Jo-Jo!" Mr. Walters held out his palm in presentation and then strode over to stand next to her. The audience wheezed a sigh of awe, as it did every day, when it saw that Josephine's face was not much higher than the tall man's knee.

"It's her! It's her! I said it would be! I knew it was!" A chorus of excited squeals rippled through the schoolgirls. Josephine did not dare to look down at them, nor up at Mr. Walters. She stared instead at the sign hanging over the door at the back of the hall:

WERE YOU ASTONISHED?
TELL A FRIEND!

"Girls! If you please!" It was the voice she dreaded most. Quite against her intentions, Josephine glanced toward it and was met with the drilling gaze of Miss MacLaren.

Later she could not remember having done her act. She could not remember parading costumes of the Great Women of History, or tapping her tambourine as a dancing Gypsy Queen, under the shrewd and steady eyes of her former employer. But her body must have performed while her mind felt frozen in panic, like a rabbit facing a rifle.

As Josephine fumbled her way off the stage, accompanied by the usual stomping cheers, she came nose to nose with Marco and Polo, who were entwined around Filipe's hips, awaiting their dramatic entrance.

The flicking tongues up close were suddenly terrifying. She had contained her fear of the wicked woman in the front row, but now she screamed, and then screamed again. When Filipe pushed past her and strutted across the stage, the whole audience screamed in a delighted echo.

Josephine, trying to swallow air, raced for the little dressing room she shared with Rosie.

"Nelly? Where's Nelly?" she cried at the door.

Rosie was heating her comb over a candle flame.

"I hasn't seen her, Jo-Jo. She wasn't mine to mind."

Rosie chuckled at her own wit and began to curl her beard.

Josephine paused in the hallway. Which way? What to do? Hide? Or run away? Her breath was coming in puffs like a toy steam engine.

"What's got into your drawers today?" Charley appeared from the wings, his pink eyes puzzled. "First you miss your cue, which is certain to tweak Mr. Walters's nose, and then you go off screaming like a brand-new baby! Do you need a tonic, Jo?"

"It's—I'm in trouble, Charley!"

"Well? Spit it out!"

"I was—the school I ran away from?" Josephine was panting. "She's here, Charley!"

"Who, Jo?"

Why couldn't he understand?

"Start again, Jo. You're not making sense."

"Then listen!" Tears were hovering. "The headmistress who hates me, she's sitting in the front row! I can't stay here! She'll find me!"

"Jo." Charley knelt in front of her, holding her shoulders. "Calm yourself. You can't go running off anywhere. You stand out like an oyster on a plate of cabbage. Why don't you just tell the old dame that you work here now, and she can jump under a horse bus for all you care?"

He didn't know about the five gold dollars. What would he think of her if he knew she was a thief?

Josephine stomped her foot. "But I'm not!"

Charley looked startled. She had spoken aloud.

"Oh, Charley," she faltered. "There's more—" She broke off as the clamor of applause from Walters Hall informed them that Filipe's turn was over.

"Yikes! I'm next!" Charley put his hands on Josephine's shoulders and whispered quick instructions.

"Just hide till she's gone, till the show's over. Tuck your wee self into a crack and wait for me."

Charley and Filipe jabbed elbows as they passed in the narrow hallway. Josephine was relieved to see that Marco and Polo were well out of reach, resting across Filipe's shoulders.

"Jo-Jo! That scream was an inspiration! Like lighting a match underneath them. Will you do it for me every time?"

She forced a smile up at him. "If you like, Filipe. If I'm still here. I mean, if Mr. Walters says I may."

"Come and help me settle the fellows for their nap," invited Filipe.

"Oh, I don't think—" Josephine hesitated. The snake cages were in Mr. Walters's office. No one would think to look for her there.

"Well, all right, Filipe."

She followed at a distance. The snakes were draped across Filipe's back, their scales glinting slightly. Her own legs were only half as thick as the pythons' coiled necks.

Mr. Walters's summer office was simply arranged. He had a desk and a chair and an oil lamp, but otherwise it was crowded with wooden packing cases. The only window provided a stream of sunshine, lighting a portable wardrobe full to bursting with his splendid coats.

Josephine halted on the threshold, her mind still in the front row of the tent. Charley said to hide. She must hide.

"I've changed my mind," she said, as Filipe opened one of the cages that sat against the far wall.

"Next time then." He was busy unwrapping the snakes and looping them into their separate berths.

He did not notice Josephine slip behind a trunk and crouch out of sight.

19
IN WHICH The Battle Lines Are Drawn

When Filipe left, whistling, he closed the door behind him. Josephine could hear a slight, snakey rustle as Marco and Polo rearranged themselves. She stood up. Maybe she could be hidden better. The row of coats hanging in the open wardrobe invited her to step inside and nestle invisibly amongst them.

A faint patter of applause told her that Charley had just finished, with his sweeping bow. That left only Eddie, exposing his peeling hide, before the finale. The finale! They were all meant to appear together at the end! She was supposed to go on again, riding on Barker's back!

But she couldn't. She just couldn't go out there. She buried her face in the soft, dark coat next to her. Hopefully, Miss MacLaren would take the girls home, and Josephine would never again have to look at her quivering neck or pouchy cheeks or beady eyes.

She imagined those eyes right now, inspecting poor, reptilian Eddie, telling her fine girls to cover their faces, pronouncing it a disgusting display. She thought of Charlotte's hateful sneers, and Nancy whining because she couldn't see properly, and then finally of Emmy's timid sympathy. She wished she could sneak out and meet Emmy somewhere before she had to go home on the train. If only they could play on the beach! Or have sweet corn and candied apples!

Josephine wished she had answered Emmy's letters. She'd been so busy and so happy, not wanting to think of MacLaren Academy. How unfair to Emmy, who must be so lonely. Josephine would write today and tell her that she'd seen her in the audience. Emmy would understand why she'd had to hide. But maybe she'd come back another time, with Margaret and My Bob; they could have a picnic, and chase the waves.

Another flurry of applause signaled Eddie's exit. By now, he would be in the wings, tearing off his yellow trousers and pulling on the red ones. They all wore red for the finale. Even Charley changed his cravat.

Rosie would have Barker in from the kennel by now.

She would look around as she buckled on the tooled leather saddle, expecting Josephine to be ready. She would send Charley to fetch her, as the music stirred into their farewell march.

What would Charley do? He might say she was sick, or he might pretend to look for her. He wouldn't have time to do much; here was the music now. She could hear the booming bass drum, even from deep in the folds of Mr. Walters's summer tweed.

Would the audience notice? Where's Little Jo-Jo? Mr. Walters would certainly notice, but he was smooth. He would drop her name from his closing salute and send the customers away, disbelieving their own eyes.

Moments later, Mr. Walters's voice raged down the corridor, accompanied by his pounding stride. Someone (was it Charley?) was trying to speak, but the master was overruling all other opinion.

"There is no excuse! I want her in my office in two minutes or she will be back in the gutter. Find her, now!"

I'm already in his office! Panic and giddiness were fighting each other inside Josephine. She was tempted to step out as the door sprang open, to see if Mr. Walters might faint with shock. But the crash with which he shut the door made her content to wait, well hidden, until the thunderstorm had passed.

Josephine could see only Mr. Walters's back from her place between the coats. It went rigid at the sound of a grating voice on the other side of the door.

"I'll thank you to tell Mr. Walters that I am here to see him." Josephine's neck prickled in recognition.

The response was muffled, but Josephine knew it was Nelly, trying to waylay Miss MacLaren.

"If he does not oblige me with an interview"—the headmistress was used to being obeyed—"I shall be compelled to call in the constabulary."

Mr. Walters turned. Josephine could see his hands freeze in midair, then clench into fists, as if preparing for battle.

There was a light tapping on the door, followed by another outburst from Miss MacLaren.

"Knock as if you mean it, you stupid woman! Is he there or not?"

"You'll be keeping a civil tongue or not taking another step, ma'am." Nelly's tone had sharpened too.

For one moment, Josephine smiled with pride, but shuddered when Mr. Walters called out, "Come in, then."

Josephine shifted slowly and slightly so that she could see a little more of the room. Nelly stood at the door, holding it open for Miss MacLaren to push past, followed by the girls in their uniform blue.

Miss MacLaren had chosen to wear a flowered dress with several flounces and was armed with a ruffled, pink parasol. Josephine thought briefly of a fat goose with a gaggle of goslings.

"Good afternoon, Madam!" Mr. Walters's voice

dripped like maple syrup, dismissing his anger temporarily. Perhaps he thought she was here to fill the position of Fat Lady.

"How can I be of assistance to you and your lovely charges?"

"My name, sir, is Miss Ethelwyn MacLaren, Director of the MacLaren Academy."

There was a wave of twittering from the girls when they heard Miss MacLaren's first name. She shot them an icicle glare, and continued.

"You are harboring a runaway from my household employ, and I wish her returned to me, at once!"

"What, Madam, are you talking about?" Mr. Walters clearly had no idea.

"I am referring, sir, to Little Jo-Jo. I have put my fine girls at great risk, coming today to this sordid establishment, and I would appreciate your swift cooperation. She belongs to me, and I want her back."

"But there must be some mistake, Madam." Mr. Walters covered his surprise with a smooth reply. "Little Jo-Jo has arrived only recently from a foreign country."

"Lies and chicanery!" Miss MacLaren was not charmed. "Do not use your schemes on me, sir!"

Josephine's view was blocked by Catherine and Harriet shuffling sideways, but she was glad not to see Mr. Walters's face while he heard this declaration.

"On the contrary, Madam, the person in question is engaged by me and shall remain so." Mr. Walters's intonation had cooled considerably.

Josephine heard a grim chuckle. The girls huddled together, expanding the view again.

"I think not, sir." Miss MacLaren was waving a piece of paper, dangerously close to Mr. Walters's moustache. "I have full proof of a transaction with her parents, giving myself ownership of the little runt, for as long as I require. This is a legal document, and you are breaking the law by employing her against my wishes!"

"And would you mind telling us just why she ran away, Miss Ethelwyn MacLaren?" Nelly sounded spitting mad. "And just what you'd do with her if she ever came back?"

The girls gasped in unison. Who would dare speak to the dreaded headmistress this way? Josephine wanted to clap her hands.

"Nelly!" Mr. Walters cautioned her.

"Mr. Walters! I am descended from one of the finest families in New York City! I am not accustomed to being addressed in this manner by ticket takers. Hand over that gruesome freak this instant, or I shall return with police officials to drag her out!"

Miss MacLaren's demeanor was slipping quickly to something less than ladylike.

"Nelly?" Mr. Walters was syrupy again. Josephine wondered what idea had struck his brain. "Nelly, please go and find the dear child. And have Filipe come along too."

Josephine nearly poked her head out in surprise. What was he up to? Filipe could be wanted for only one thing. The snakes.

20
IN WHICH Things Turn Ugly

Josephine had never heard the cluster of ninnies so silent as when they were waiting for her to show up to her doom. She could see Miss MacLaren's fleshy fingers smoothing down the flounces of her skirt, trying to calm her agitation.

Mr. Walters began to hum. To hum! A sinister signal indeed. The discomfort of everyone in the room was elevated by the carefree, tuneless burr coming from Mr. Walters's throat.

Nelly was back in the doorway.

"Jo is not in her dressing room, sir," she announced in an even clip. "My Charley says she was poorly and may have gone back to the boarding house."

Josephine wondered if Charley had told his mother the truth. From her voice, she guessed yes, though Nelly needed no further reason to despise Miss MacLaren than her insults had already provided.

"What trick is this? You've hidden her somewhere! Do you take me for a fool?" The veins on Miss MacLaren's nose were turning darker as she warmed up for another tirade. The girls pressed themselves against the crates.

She'll burst her corset, with us all watching, thought Josephine.

"Did you want for me to come in here, Mr. Walters?" Filipe hovered in the doorway, eyeing the crowded room.

The girls stared at the snake trainer as if he were an exotic animal, with his tawny skin and shining mane of black hair. Josephine could see Harriet nudge Catherine, with a smirk. They had never been so near to anyone so handsome.

"Yes, Filipe. I believe it's time for you to be back on exhibition in the main promenade. Is it Marco's turn? Or Polo's?"

Filipe hesitated and then apparently caught on to what was desired of him. He shimmied past the schoolgirls, perhaps closer than he needed to, and knelt before Marco's cage. Not until that moment had any of the visitors even noticed that they were sharing the room with reptiles.

Catherine was the first to realize what must be in the cage. She started to moan before Filipe had even turned around, gripping Marco awkwardly. There was a group intake of horrified breath as the snake swayed.

"Usually, I wear him, no trouble," apologized Filipe, with a lopsided smile. "But he is maybe nervous with so many pretty girls watching." He fumbled to lift the snake into place across his shoulders, but it twisted with a strong tug and plunged to the floor.

Josephine's yelp was easily lost in the screeching wails that filled the room. Marco shot across the floor, straight for Miss MacLaren's white, buttoned shoes. The headmistress didn't wait to see her fate. She swooned, with a whimper, and crashed to the ground, like a harpooned whale. Marco sideswiped past her, seeking cover.

Harriet and Felicia fainted in the same moment, falling over each other and blocking the doorway. Marco was trapped, and so was everyone else. In a chaotic uproar of grabbing and shoving, yanking and howling, the remaining students of MacLaren Academy tried to leave the room.

Amidst the knuckles and knees, Josephine could see Emmy crouched against a packing crate, sobbing into her hands. Filipe was on all fours, beckoning to Marco, who had found sanctuary behind the wardrobe.

"Do something to revive these bodies," commanded Mr. Walters.

"With pleasure, sir!" Nelly clasped the handle of the fire bucket which stood next to the door. She flung water on the slack face of Miss MacLaren, who sat up spluttering. She had barely taken a breath before she was on her feet and babbling hysterically.

"Girls! Gather yourselves, girls! Get out! Get out! Who's this? Harriet? Smack her! Wake her up! Get out! Run! Felicia? Up, girl! Run! Run!"

And run they did. After several collisions, and more squawking than inside a henhouse, the girls scurried down the corridor without looking back.

But Miss MacLaren paused in the doorway to point a threatening finger at Mr. Walters. She could not disguise the wobble in her voice.

"I'll be back. And you will deliver my property, or I shall expose you for the lowdown fraud that you are!" She turned, with a final notion of majesty, and waddled quickly after her charges.

Mr. Walters sat in the chair with an emphatic sigh. Josephine unclenched her fingers, feeling stiff and shaken. If only they would all leave so that she could move again. She saw Nelly lean over Filipe on the floor.

"Is Marco all right?" she asked.

Filipe pulled him gently out of his hiding place, clicking his tongue as if he were cajoling a toddler.

"He will recover with no complaint."

"Filipe!" Mr. Walters stood up to congratulate him. "You did a fine job! I will remember that on pay day!"

"Oh, thank you, Mr. Walters, sir!"

"Now, off you go. They'll be missing you out front."

Nelly stood aside to let Filipe past. Marco hung limply from his shoulder. He would not appear too menacing this afternoon.

Still in her hiding place, Josephine was suddenly aware of being unbearably hot. Her scalp was aflame. She was still wearing Cleopatra's wig! She tore it off and dropped it silently at her feet.

"Nelly, I see why you might wish to protect Josephine from that bloated cow, but there is no excuse for her to miss a performance, certainly not without explanation, and I—"

"I don't know where she is, sir. Charley says he told her to wait, but she's gone. She must have been that afraid."

"Indeed?" Mr. Walters's voice had gone flat. "Who's on duty at the ticket booth, Nelly?"

"My Charley's there now."

"He should be on exhibit. And you should be taking the money. That's what I pay you for. Go."

Josephine could hear Nelly's voice, coming in from the hallway. "All I know is, she's a wee thing and shouldn't be out there on her own." The door closed.

Mr. Walters was back near his desk, where Josephine couldn't see him. What if he stayed there for hours? Wasn't he going to look for her? Or send out a search party? She heard papers shifting. What if he chose to work instead?

She felt as though she was under six blankets. How much longer could she stand it? Her neck was hot, her forehead was perspiring, her nose tickled. Oh, no! She was going to sneeze! She clamped her mouth closed and pinched her nose and pressed her tongue against her teeth. She couldn't sneeze! Not now!

Ahhh. The sneeze went away. But how long would it be before another one came along? Oh, and how hot it was!

Suddenly her anguish ended. Mr. Walters was on his feet and out the door. Maybe he'd gone to summon the policemen who patrolled the beach. She had better move quickly. She stepped out from between the coats and fanned her skirt away from her legs. Even that small breeze was a relief. She lifted her damp hair and shook her head back and forth, cooling the back of her neck.

Without warning, the door swung open again. She was caught. Mr. Walters was consulting his watch and didn't even see her, in the first second. It was when he slipped the watch back into his vest pocket and adjusted the chain that he noticed her.

They both stood frozen. They could have been the same height, their eyes were so steadily locked.

"Josephine."

"Mr. Walters."

"You have caused immeasurable trouble." He was eerily calm. "But I suppose you know that. Have you been here all along?"

"Yes, sir."

"Marco performed admirably, did he not?"

"Yes, sir."

"And I see that the door to his cage is still open."

"Sir?"

"It is a strict rule that Exhibitions never miss an appearance. I expect you to be onstage at the required times, including five o'clock this afternoon. You undoubtedly wish to avoid the unpleasant Miss MacLaren. Thus, as a reminder of the regulations, and for your own protection, I must request that you get into Marco's cage."

21
IN WHICH Josephine
Is Teased by Danger

No amount of pleading would change his
mind. In the end, Mr. Walters held Josephine by the shoulder and forced her into Marco's cage,
pushing her head in first with his huge hand. The train
of her Cleopatra shift was caught in the door when he
closed the latch.

She hadn't tried to bite him, which is what she was
bursting to do. She hadn't even screamed for help, not
wanting his huge hand clamped over her mouth. Her
throat was clogged. Every hair on her body was bristling
with rage. She was too small to fight back.

Mr. Walters selected a brown coat from the wardrobe
and draped it over the cage before leaving the room
without another word.

Josephine huddled in darkness, listening to her own
ragged breathing. She could smell snake, swampy and
dry at the same time. Polo moved in the next door cage,
sending goose bumps up her arms. She had enough room
to stand up straight, with her head brushing the ceiling,
but she sank into the corner, hugging herself.

Josephine wished she could be like Alice, in the book
about Wonderland. If only I had a cake, she thought,
that said "Eat Me." Then she could grow and grow until

she was big enough to stomp on anyone who had insulted her.

She wanted to kill Mr. Walters. She wanted to poison his porridge and poke him with knives. How could he do this? She hadn't run away from him. She hadn't missed the finale on purpose. She would never do that except that Miss MacLaren was there, waiting to pounce. He should know by now that she was reliable. He wouldn't even listen. Her fingernails were digging into her palms.

How dare he push her! How dare he! Into a cage! She wanted to kill him. She wanted to burn his whiskers and slash his fancy coats with a pair of scissors. How could anyone put a person in a cage? The answer hit Josephine like a hard stick. To him it was a simple matter of commerce. She was a valuable exhibit, not a person at all.

Josephine's eyes were hot with tears. She grasped the wooden struts of her prison and shook them.

Wait a minute! This was a snake cage, not meant to hold people. Snakes can't think, to get out of things. Josephine's tears were dry before she had finished the thought. People with big brains and small hands can get out of cages made for snakes. The door wasn't even locked. It was closed with a latch on the outside.

Josephine slipped her hand between the bars and felt for the little lever. Sure enough, it moved when she jiggled it. She bit her lip and told her heart to stop hammering. If she could lift the bar far enough, it might slide out of place.

Then, from the corridor. "Come right in here, sir." Nelly's voice! But clearly speaking to a stranger.

"I'll fetch Mr. Walters in a wink." The office door opened, and footsteps scuffled on the threshold.

"You can sit yourself down, sir. Oh, perhaps not. There's only the one chair. And that's his."

Josephine pulled her hand back through the struts, even though it was masked by the drape of Mr. Walters's coat. She couldn't tell Nelly she was here until she knew who was with her.

It was a man with a good-humored chuckle.

"Then I can take my pick of packing crates?"

Nelly laughed too. "Make yourself at home! Here's Mr. Walters coming now."

"Nelly! What are you doing in my—" Mr. Walters's edgy tone changed as he must have seen the guest. "Oh. Good afternoon, sir. What can I do for you?"

"This is Mr. Gideon Smyth, sir. He's the gentleman reporter from the *Tribune,* in the city. The one who wrote the lovely notice about Josephine."

"Indeed?"

"Happy to meet you again, Mr. Walters. I'd like to do an additional piece on the little lady. How she's doing on the job, is she popular, how much she eats in a day. A personal look, so to speak."

Josephine stopped breathing to listen.

"Can we talk somewhere else?" Mr. Walters was being polite, but strained. "As you can see, my office is lacking any civilized amenities at the moment."

"Oh, heck, I don't care a sweet fig about that. I'm comfortable anywhere."

Josephine grinned in the dark. She knew that Mr. Walters must be squirming.

"I'd like to interview her," Mr. Smyth continued, in a voice full of lazy confidence. "Put it down in her own words maybe. I notice she's not out front there. Any chance I could have a few minutes with her after I've talked to you?"

Josephine almost laughed out loud.

"This is not the best time," said Mr. Walters abruptly. "She has to be onstage in . . ." There was a clink, as he consulted his watch. ". . . in twenty-two minutes, so I must insist that you come another day."

"Oh, I'll just wait until the next show is over. I'd like to see the little lady in action anyway. She's really something special in my estimation." Mr. Smyth's trick of being pleasantly persistent was wearing down the opposition.

"Can I get you something to drink, Mr. Smyth?" Nelly summoned her manners. "While you're waiting? A lemonade maybe?"

"He's not waiting!"

Then Mr. Walters caught himself. "Not in here certainly. Nelly, get back to your duties. I'll give Mr. Smyth a personal tour of the museum while he's waiting. Come along!"

"Mr. Walters, sir? There was a small matter of something being misplaced earlier on?" Nelly was trying not to say the wrong thing in front of the newspaperman.

"That's all taken care of, Nelly. Don't worry yourself about it. Please assume your post at the entrance. The five o'clock show will go according to plan." Did Josephine imagine that he spoke more loudly to say this?

She counted a full minute after their footsteps faded. Then her fingers rapidly unfastened the latch. Mr. Walters's coat hung across the door, preventing it from swinging open, but Josephine squeezed through, pushing the garment out of her way. She stood, then hopped up and down, shaking her hands and feet. She fancied she was a cup of ginger beer, full of bubbles that tingled on the inside. She wanted to shout aloud.

"Too bad for you, you slithery old stinker," she mocked Polo. His scales rasped against the side of his cage as he rolled over. "I'm free, and you're not!"

But not altogether. She was still in Mr. Walters's office and still in his museum. And somewhere outside was Miss MacLaren, looking to capture her. And now there was Mr. Gideon Smyth as well, though he seemed much nicer than the other two. He might even help her, if she could figure out what she wanted help with.

Josephine brushed off the silky folds of her Egyptian shift. There was no point in trying to run away or hide again right now. She would perform in the second matinee and consult with Charley afterward. Together they would think of something clever. In the meantime, she'd better change her costume if she was going to appear at five o'clock.

"Good-bye, Polo. I won't be missing you."

She crossed the slanting, sunlit patch on the floor and peered down the hall. Within seconds, she had crept to her empty dressing room. Rosie must be on exhibition, but the lavender scent of her beard balm lingered in the air. Barker was asleep on his cushion in the corner.

Seconds more, and Josephine was wearing the white ball gown of Mary Todd Lincoln. As she fastened the tiny pearl buttons, she thought of Mr. Walters's face when he returned to find her in the snake cage. The wicked bully! Well, she just wouldn't be there. And when she appeared on stage a few minutes later, she meant to give his heart the jump of its life.

Lifting her skirt, like a lady about to dance a gavotte, Josephine made her way toward the tented theater. Charley and Filipe would be at the front entrance by now, tantalizing the crowds leaving the beach, enticing them inside for one more thrill before they caught the train back to the city. And Nelly would be smiling at the entrance, taking their money as quickly as she could, putting the coins into the pocket of her apron.

"There she is, Constable! There's the scrawny runt now!"

Josephine staggered at the sound of Miss MacLaren's holler. Spinning around, she saw the headmistress, red in the face and waddling just in front of seven panting schoolgirls. Close behind them was a policeman, wielding a wooden nightstick.

22
IN WHICH Josephine Is Surrounded

There she is, Constable! Arrest her at once!"

Josephine turned to flee, not thinking about her chances. But before she could take a step, she was confronted by Mr. R. J. Walters and a shaggy-haired stranger, who must be Mr. Gideon Smyth. They appeared from the theater tent, roused by the commotion.

She was surrounded.

"I knew you were hiding her!" Miss MacLaren crowed in triumph. "You see that, Constable? She was here all along!"

Josephine lifted her chin to meet Mr. Walters's stare with all the calm she could muster. In the passing of a second, she saw him master his shock.

"I tried to stop them!" Nelly appeared in the hall, with Charley at her heels. "Mr. Walters, I tried. But she had the policeman, there wasn't much I could do.

"Oh! Dear Jo! Where have you been?" Nelly pushed her way through the press of girls, knocking straw hats askew in her hurry.

"Nelly!" cried Josephine, not expecting the lump that rose in her throat. "I was—"

"You missed the finale of the first show! We couldn't

find you. It's nearly time for the second." She knelt on the planked floor and swept Josephine into her arms.

Josephine clung back, not ready to speak. Charley patted her head with awkward strokes.

"We were almighty worried, Jo."

"Constable, I demand that you end this display of sentimental eyewash. Arrest the girl as a thief and a runaway!"

Miss MacLaren lunged forward and plucked Josephine right out of Nelly's embrace. Nelly pulled her back, and for a moment, Josephine was yanked like a sausage between two hungry dogs. Emmy began to scream.

"Well, now, this ain't the way I aim to see ladies actin'." The policeman's gravelly voice called everyone to attention. He motioned for Josephine's release.

Nelly loosened her hold and stood up, brushing down her dress. Emmy tried to push forward, but Miss MacLaren snatched her collar and twisted her back. Josephine, trembling and sniffing, stepped sideways to avoid Miss MacLaren. Charley quietly took her hand and wrapped her fingers in the warmth of his.

"We're havin' ourselves a dispute," said the policeman, with a chuckle, addressing himself to Mr. Walters. "I think we should step outside to discuss the matter."

"Indeed, my dear Officer Beale. Please lead the way. We shall follow you to the main entrance."

Mr. Walters was mindful of his audience. Josephine

noticed that Mr. Gideon Smyth was leaning against the wall, trying to find the best light for writing in his notepad. Charley held on to her hand, and she found that Emmy was daring to hold the other.

But Catherine and Felicia were close behind.

"Sneak!" they hissed. They yanked Emmy away and pushed her out of Jo's reach.

The parade attracted much attention as it straggled through the museum. An eager officer of the law, a huffing schoolmistress, a clatch of children in uniform, an albino, a midget, a mother, a reporter, and an impresario! Filipe and Eddie and Rosie all watched in bemusement from their posts. The paying customers were agog with curiosity.

Mr. Walters, bringing up the rear of the train, was quick to see the possibilities of such an opportunity.

"Ladies and gentlemen!" he boomed, as he traipsed to the portal overlooking the beach. "The five o'clock performance will be postponed by half an hour due to police activity in the neighborhood. By coming to the theater tent at half after five, you will be among the few to know the outcome!"

He ordered Nelly to remain inside, to sell extra tickets for the impromptu presentation.

"But I want to look out for Jo, sir!" she protested.

Mr. Walters, in full view of Charley and Josephine, winked at Nelly and removed a fold of paper money from her apron pocket.

"Don't you worry about our Jo. Let's see if I can't talk

sense to Officer Beale," he said, with a smile. "But we'll draw a bit more of a crowd first." He strode out to the esplanade and recommenced his ballyhoo.

"It's never too late for surprises, ladies and gentlemen! Here at the Museum of Earthly—"

"He's going to bribe the constable!" whispered Josephine. She didn't like the feel of it. "He can't do that!"

"Why not?" Charley shrugged his shoulders. "That's the way it's done. Spondulicks, remember?"

"If he pays off the constable, he'll think I'm obliged to him. He'll think I owe him something!"

Unless he could be reminded that he owed her. He shouldn't forget the insult of the snake cage.

"There must be another way out of this!" Josephine tapped the side of her head, trying to shake loose a good idea.

"—an entire world of Nature's Marvels awaits behind these doors!" Mr. Walters continued to enchant the onlookers.

"Constable?" Miss MacLaren had put up her pink parasol, giving her the look of a frosted teacake. "Are you going to permit him to strut about in this manner? I want him placed under arrest as well as the little freak."

Mr. Walters's expression became more grave at once.

"The woman is mad!" muttered Nelly.

The schoolgirls gasped.

Josephine rocked on her toes. Miss MacLaren really did have a nerve!

"Well, sir?" said the constable. "We've all heard the lady's complaint. What've you got to say?"

"I have tolerated this woman's behavior long enough. I would like to know the nature of the accusations against myself and my colleague." He indicated Josephine with a nod.

Charley squeezed Josephine's hand. She knew he was saying, "Colleague?" with his pink eyeballs rolling to Heaven.

"That puny thing has been a charity case in my fine Academy for five years." Miss MacLaren didn't look at Josephine while she spoke. "Through the goodness of my heart, I saved her from a life of neglect. Despite her incompetence, she was permitted to perform the occasional chore to allow for her pride."

Josephine's heart was beating louder than the lies. Emmy, squeezed between Harriet and Felicia, shook her head like a broken puppet.

"I fed her and clothed her and gave her an excellent education. And she repaid me by stealing! She sneaked into my study and stole my money before creeping away into the night!"

Nancy and Charlotte and the others were smirking, as if knowing all the time that she was a criminal. Josephine's face was hot, scorched by all the eyes staring indignantly. She felt her feet burning inside the shoes she'd bought with her gold dollars. Emmy looked horrified. Mr. Gideon Smyth was writing. Mr. Walters seemed intrigued. Charley squinted in surprise, disbelieving the impossible. The constable looked bored.

"Well, Miss?"

"I only took my wages that were owing. I wasn't a resident in her stinking Academy. I was a slave."

Miss MacLaren gasped and fanned her face with a glove.

"And there aren't allowed to be slaves anymore, thanks to Mr. Abraham Lincoln. People who work should be paid. I was a hard worker every day."

Josephine saw Emmy's head nodding up and down.

"They weren't good to me," she continued, in her husky voice. "Miss MacLaren is saying untruths. I got beaten. The new cook beat me. So I left. And I took my wages with me."

Mr. Gideon Smyth's pencil skittered back and forth across the page as Miss MacLaren screeched her response.

"Don't you get uppity with me! I sent your wages to your parents every year, as agreed, so what you took was out-and-out stealing. Do you hear that, Constable? She has confessed to a whole platoon of witnesses!"

Officer Beale shifted uncomfortably, as if his trousers were buttoned on too tight. He seemed to examine Josephine from under his shaggy eyebrows before he cocked his head toward Mr. Walters.

"What say you to that, eh?"

Mr. Walters managed an indulgent chuckle.

"The problem is simply one of misunderstanding!" He caressed his moustache, as though the solution should now be clear to everyone.

"If you would let me have a private word, my dear man." Mr. Walters draped an arm across the constable's shoulders. Josephine saw the fingers of his other hand clutching the folded money he had taken from Nelly's apron. She had to do something!

"Excuse me!" Josephine felt a tremor of power rise through her spine. She knew she had to stop him.

"Mr. Walters is right. It's all just a misunderstanding. I took that money by mistake. Miss MacLaren wants it back. She doesn't really want me for a servant anymore. I'm too small and not very satisfactory. Isn't that the impression you got, Mr. Smyth?"

Josephine was depending on luck. Would the reporter help her now? His eyebrows were arched in admiration, giving her the wits to go on.

"Did you meet Mr. Gideon Smyth?" She addressed the headmistress for the first time. "Mr. Smyth is a reporter. He's here to write down everything about me. I'm pretty sure he put down the part about when I was beaten by your cook." Miss MacLaren raised a hand in denial and simpered at Mr. Smyth.

"And he might put down all manner of things, about anything I might care to tell him, about any of the places I've worked, or things that might have been done to me."

Now she was looking Mr. Walters straight in the eye.

"So I know that Mr. Walters will be happy to pay

Miss MacLaren the five dollars I took, and then we'll all be settled up. I even think he has money in his pocket right now."

Mr. Walters was truly flummoxed. Josephine bit the inside of her cheek so he wouldn't see the grin she was sucking on while he reluctantly counted out the money and pressed it into Miss MacLaren's white glove.

Surrounded by a keenly curious crowd, Miss MacLaren had no option but to accept the funds. She tugged on the strings of her purse and put the money inside, with her mouth shriveled up like a walnut.

"Well, now," said Officer Beale, "that's over then."

But Mr. Walters wasn't quite finished.

"Perhaps you would be so kind," he said, with a theatrical wave of his hand, "dear Officer Beale, to accompany Miss MacLaren and her charges to the train station?"

He shook the constable's hand with a carefully hidden gift in his palm. Only someone of Josephine's height could swear to the exchange. Mr. Walters clearly recognized the usefulness of a contented police patrol.

Mr. Gideon Smyth bowed low to Josephine.

"I'd like to have a word with you, after the show, perhaps?"

"Oh, yes, sir."

"Not today, my friend." Mr. Walters swiftly placed himself between Josephine and the newspaperman. "The child has tired herself out and will need to rest. Come another time."

Mr. Gideon Smyth saluted Josephine with a wink. He tucked his notebook into his coat pocket and trundled off.

As Miss MacLaren convened her flock, Josephine searched for Emmy to signal a farewell, but now she was out of sight amidst her classmates. Josephine's heart turned over in regret that she hadn't had a chance to say good-bye.

IN WHICH Josephine Plans for the Future

Mr. Walters hustled his exhibitions back indoors to perform their overdue matinee. Josephine did not speak to her employer, nor did he approach her. It seemed they both knew a truce had been called and would leave the peace conference until a later time.

Onstage Josephine felt cheered by her admirers. Whatever had happened behind the scenes, she was still queen of her audience. But how long could she rule?

Following the performance, Josephine went straight to her platform in the main promenade. She was still ajitter, reliving the afternoon's drama. Miss MacLaren was like an invading dragon, breathing fire from the moat. Mr. Walters was even worse, the duplicitous knight inside the castle walls, awaiting his chance to confine the queen.

Finally the closing bell sounded, and lingering patrons trailed out of the building. The walls were instantly ghostly in the feeble light.

Josephine climbed down her ladder, promising to meet Charley outside to walk back to the boarding house together. The door to her dressing room was ajar. Was that singing coming from within? It surely wasn't Rosie. She had a voice like a nanny goat.

Josephine peeked around the door. Barker lay asleep on his tattered horsehair cushion. And Emmy sat next to him, with her hand resting between his ears.

"Emmy!"

"Josephine!"

Josephine threw herself around her friend's neck where she sat, pushing her off balance and across Barker's back. They laughed as the dog snorted and opened an eye, but he didn't seem to mind being a mattress.

"What are you doing here?" Josephine gasped.

"I couldn't bear to go back to school, it's been awful! Miss MacLaren is in such a temper, she made us come to find you, saying all the time you were ungrateful and stupid, and if you were going to exploit yourself, you should have gone uptown to the mighty P. T. Barnum. She didn't say about the stolen money. Oh, Josephine! How did you dare!"

"I just had to. That's where you found me, remember? But now you've scarpered school! Talk about daring!"

"I've been sitting here waiting for you, thinking of nothing but my father's face when he's notified I'm gone, the way his eyes go crossed when he's angry. I can't decide if he'll kill me for running off, or kill Miss MacLaren for losing me!"

"Probably both, but we'll say it was her fault. Dragging her fine girls to such a dubious den! Whatever was she thinking!"

That started them laughing all over again, trying Barker's patience to the limit. He heaved himself up and gave a good shake just as Rosie came through the door. Barker greeted his mistress with a plaintive whine and a limp wag of his tail.

"Hello, Rosie," said Josephine, knowing that the Bearded Lady's brain was as thick as a Bible. She wouldn't realize that anything was amiss. "This is my friend Emmy. She's been watching Barker sleep."

"Ah, now, that's nice. Come along, my pet, time to go home." Barker shuffled to her side, and they departed.

"Oh! Jo-Jo!" Rosie poked her whiskery face around the door. "I near forgot. Charley's waiting on you, with Nelly. By the oyster boys, he said."

Josephine and Emmy looked at each other, suddenly serious.

"What'll I do?"

"Come home with us," declared Josephine. "Nelly'll help think of a plan. She's Charley's ma, but she's not a regular mother; she's completely trustworthy. Come on. Let's go meet them, and you can sleep with me tonight."

"Oh, Jo! What have you done?" Nelly was more upset to see Emmy than Josephine had expected.

"Emmy's company!" protested Josephine. "She's my friend!"

"She'll be missed at once!" cried Nelly. "They'll be back to find her!"

"I didn't think of that," admitted Josephine.

Emmy hung her head.

"I didn't mean trouble for anyone," she said, "I just wanted to see Josephine."

"You're a skedaddler!" blurted Charley.

"Close it, Charley!" Josephine shushed him, but he was irrepressible.

"You weren't content to steal money from the old bat, Jo? Now you're taking her pupils too?"

Nelly swatted her son lightly on the head, told him to button his lip, and announced that she would hold a family meeting in her bed chamber after supper was eaten and cleared away.

They introduced Emmy to Hilda as a friend who would be staying the night. Although the landlady grumbled that she preferred to have a little notice, she ladled out enough fish stew for everyone.

Nelly postponed any serious conversation until they were alone upstairs. Other years, Nelly had shared a room with Charley. But this season, Josephine slept in the second bed in Nelly's room, and Charley had a cot in the alcove by the sitting room.

It was the first bed of Josephine's life. The first that she could remember anyway. At the school, she had slept next to the stove on a straw pallet. In Nelly's apartment on Forsyth Street, she had only a folded blanket.

The ceremony of hauling herself up to lie upon the real mattress and to stroke the battered brass knobs on the corners of the bedstead was a nightly pleasure that had lost none of its novelty. And as Josephine's body did not begin to fill the space, of course there was room for a friend.

"We've got a few decisions to make," Nelly announced, as Charley settled himself on the floor at her feet. Emmy and Josephine sat cross-legged on the bed. "Emmy, you'll not be staying more than a night with us—"

"Oh, but Nelly!" Josephine was alarmed.

"Mrs. O'Dooley! I can't go back to school!"

"Miss MacLaren would chew her up and spit out the bones," added Josephine.

"I won't take you to school, Emmy. Now that you've told me your sister is married to Robert Dixon, I'll take you in to the Half-Dollar Saloon. He was always a gentleman when I worked there with him."

"That's a good idea!" Emmy sighed with relief.

"No, it's not," said Josephine. "They'll just send her back to Miss MacLaren, and she'll get twenty licks with the leather!"

Emmy shuddered, but Nelly ignored them both.

"What happens after that is up to her family, Jo."

"But—"

"There's nothing to say 'but' about. If she stays here any longer, we'll all be in terrible trouble. There'll be policemen and reporters and nosy do-gooders. Emmy's father is a powerful man. We could be arrested! Or the museum closed down. Think how worried her parents must be tonight."

"I'm sure they won't know until tomorrow, Nelly," Emmy piped up. "Miss MacLaren won't want to report until she has to. The school is not on the telephone yet. She'll have to wait for the post."

"All the same, Emmy. You're still a child. Your future has to be decided by your parents. And I'm sure it will be well taken care of."

Emmy nodded, chewing on the tip of her braid. "You're right, Mrs. O'Dooley."

"I'm still a child too," said Josephine, pouting.

"Aye, but you're a child without parents. You've had to make choices for yourself a wee bit sooner than Emmy here. And you've done pretty well for the most part."

"You're very brave, Josephine," said Emmy. "I could never—"

"Maybe I don't like doing all the thinking for myself."

"It's much better that way, Jo." Charley sounded as though he knew for certain. "Do you think I'm listening for Mr. Walters, or even Nelly, to tell me what to do with my life?"

"Yes, Charley, I do. We're all listening to Mr. Walters, as a matter of fact. You've been listening to him for more than half your life!"

"Well, he is the boss, Jo," Charley admitted, "but not forever. I plan to run my life the way I want it to be, not as anyone else decides for me."

"That sounds very grand, Charley," said Nelly softly. "Now, isn't it a good thing you're not needing to run anything for a time yet?"

Josephine didn't like to hear him bragging. "That's a lot of fat talk, Charley. Run your life in which direction? You won't be the Albino Boy forever, you know. You're fourteen years old. But you aren't learning a trade to take you anywhere different. Do you want to grow up to be the Albino Man?"

"That's what I'll be anyway, you daft girl! This is who I am!"

"Oh, please!" cried Emmy. "Please don't shout."

Josephine lowered her voice, but kept on. "What kind of life is that?"

"Is it better to be 'the Albino coal hauler' that everyone snickers at behind my back, or 'the Albino coach driver'?" Charley turned on Josephine. "Do you want to be 'the midget in the sewing factory'? Or 'the midget who cooks the hot dogs at Feltman's'?"

"That's enough, Charley." Nelly's voice was firm. She put up her hand to signal an end to the conversation. "We won't have any more of this."

Charley's pale cheeks were flushed with the first color

Josephine had ever seen in them. He ignored his mother and continued to rail at Josephine. "Do you think you'll start growing all of a sudden when you're not a child anymore? Even if you quit being Little Jo-Jo, you'll be a midget until the day they find you dead in your teeny little bed!"

"Oh, no!" Emmy's hand flew to her mouth.

"Charley!" Nelly stood up and turned her son toward the door.

Charley held his palms to his cheeks, as if feeling their heat.

"I'm to bed," he said.

Josephine's eyes prickled with tears as he left the room. What had she said to make Charley so angry? She'd only said what he knew to be true. That Mr. Walters owned them both. That there might be a better life out there somewhere.

"I think we should all be getting to bed," said Nelly gently. She sat next to Josephine on the quilt and put an arm about her shoulder.

"You have plenty of time to worry about the future, Jo. And no one is sending you out on your own, now that we've found you." Nelly was warm, and she smelled faintly of apples. Josephine leaned against her, inhaling the calm.

"Emmy, however, will have to be going tomorrow." Nelly was regretful, but left no opening for protest. Emmy bowed her head, knowing she had no choice.

"I'll take her into the city in the morning, while you

and Charley get yourselves to work. When we hear how it all shakes out, maybe Margaret can bring her again, for a visit, on a Sunday."

24

Josephine Can't Sleep

Is Charley always so forceful?" Emmy asked in a whisper. "It seemed a dreadful argument."

"We never had a disagreement before. Only teasing, is all." Josephine was quiet a moment, getting used to having a confidante. "I'm all twisted up inside, not feeling sure how we'll settle it."

"Oh, you'll fix things," said Emmy. "I can see you're the best of friends, really."

"Do the girls do this at school?" asked Josephine. "Talk at night in the dormitory?"

"Not to me," said Emmy. "I have the corner bed, so I'm out of the way. I do hear them whispering, though."

"I never slept next to a person before," confessed Josephine. "I don't know if I wriggle."

"I hope you don't mind me saying," said Emmy, "that you're just about the size of my best doll, Belinda. She sits on the chest at the end of my bed at home. I'm not supposed to touch her really, her clothes are ever so fancy. You're better than a doll, of course. Smarter."

"People at the museum think I'm a doll sometimes," said Josephine. "They think it's a trick of some kind, that I can move and talk. So I don't mind you saying it, in a nice way. But it's an odd thing; all the day long, I'm next to big folk, or regular folk, I guess you'd say. The size of them is so familiar to me, sometimes it's a surprise when I see my own hand or my own foot. Then I remember again that I'm small."

Emmy was quiet. Then she tucked her arm around Josephine and, soon after, dozed off. Josephine lay still, cherishing the warmth of Emmy's body. She could hear Nelly's steady breath from the other bed.

Josephine, however, was jumpy as a grasshopper. For a while, she followed Emmy's breathing, willing herself to go to sleep along with her. But finally she climbed carefully out from under her friend's arm and hopped to the ground. She kept hearing Charley shouting at her, telling her things she wasn't liking to listen to.

Silently she dressed and crept down the stairs, carrying her stockings and shoes. She would sit outside for a bit. Her thoughts were flitting around inside her head like flies in a sugar bowl.

The front door croaked faintly when she opened it and closed too quickly, with a thump, behind her. But no one called out, so Josephine sat on the doorstep to pull on her stockings and shoes. It was true, what Charley said. She would always be a midget. She would always wear stockings that could fit a cat. She would always have to reach for things that other folk just took.

Josephine tipped back her head to see the sky. She spent so much of each day bending her neck to look up, it should have snapped in two by now! She stepped into the street and turned, without hesitating, toward the ocean.

She hadn't been outside alone after dark since her departure from the MacLaren Academy. Hilda's little road was tucked away from the bustle, but as Josephine ventured farther, she discovered all manner of person, plying all manner of trade. The streets in Coney Island were as wide awake at night as in the city.

Boisterous customers spilled out of the taverns into the street, singing or fighting or strutting. The smell of beer drenched the air like mist. Rough men, selling everything from cigars and wagers to whiskey and knives, were stationed whichever way she looked.

Dodging the action, Josephine made her way to the beach, where even the water was tranquil tonight. The surface reflected stars and moonlight in glimmering splinters. A girl might glide across it, collecting gold dust on the soles of her feet.

How much had changed since her first glimpse of this splendid ocean! She had begun with such faith that Mr. Walters's promise of happiness was moments away from becoming true. And it did come true for a while, didn't it? She liked her dresses, and the pounding applause. She liked the two gold dollars she plucked from Mr. Walters's large, flat palm every Saturday night.

Couldn't she have those things without feeling

obliged to her employer? Without the fear of being caged or scolded? Though Mr. Walters had once promised her a family, it was not the museum where she felt at home. As much as she liked the other Astonishments, they were all too used to being on the outside of life. And Mr. Walters encouraged them to be peculiar.

Josephine had found her family with Nelly and Charley, not in the museum. She wanted to keep the family and change the home. Charley was right about deciding for herself.

Just as she thought his name, Josephine saw Charley's form strolling across the sand, with his skin alight beneath the moon.

"I heard you go out," he explained, not looking at her. "I thought I'd better follow in case you found trouble."

"And what would you do with trouble if it found me?" sassed Josephine. "With you being blind as a mole? It'll be me leading you home by the hand."

She watched for his smile, but she could see he wasn't giving in just yet.

"I like to go out at night," he said, almost to himself. "There's no sun to worry about, frying me up like bacon."

Josephine stared out across the water, waiting to talk.

"Charley—" she began.

"Jo—" said Charley at the same moment.

"You go ahead first," said Josephine.

"I only wanted to say . . ." Charley hesitated. "I only

think you should get used to being little, Jo. So's you can settle down and make use of it."

"I do know I'll always be small," said Josephine. "I'm not a ninny. But it seems wrong somehow to pretend it's a skill of some kind. Just to use the thing you were born with and not put any effort or brains into it. Like being born pretty or rich and that being the end of it."

Charley shook his head impatiently. "Don't you see, Jo? It's just the opposite. Outsiders like us, we need extra wits and extra courage to stay the way we're born. We have to be who we are and hold our heads up at the same time. Can you see that?"

"Yes, I can see that. And I'm ready for it, I really am. Only I'm not staying with Mr. Walters anymore. Because he thinks of it as business, and for us, it's our life. You should be the boss, Charley, you understand."

Charley reached out his hand and rested it on Josephine's shoulder.

"We could do it, Jo, just us, with Nelly to manage things, and maybe one or two others."

"Maybe."

"We could move around like gypsies. See the world a bit too."

"I'd like that, Charley. I'd like to see what's on the other side of that ocean." She took a deep breath of the salty night air and blew it out in a happy gust. She opened her arms wide, knowing suddenly there was a whole world waiting out there for her.

"Do you suppose there's other midgets right here in Coney Island?" she wondered.

"Walters' Museum boasts to have the only one out here," said Charley, "but there's plenty in the city, I'll stake my hair."

"You can keep your hair, Charley. You'd be a fright, bald. I just was curious, is all. Did you ever meet another albino?"

"I saw one once in a traveling show. Nelly took me, thinking I'd like to see. It was a Wild Man Albino, with his hair all tangly, and him growling like a raging bear from behind a screen made of a fishing net. But he took one look at me and dropped to his knees, like he was ashamed of himself."

Charley brushed a hand over his face, remembering.

"He whispered to me, real quiet and calm, so's nobody else could hear, he said, 'I've the heart of a gentleman, Boy, not the savage you see. Don't ignore your heart, Boy, if you want a moment's peace.' That's what he said."

"That's hard to do," said Josephine. She slipped her hand into Charley's thin, white one. "Especially at the Museum of Earthly Astonishments."

"What we have to remember is, there's things on this earth more astonishing than the color of a person's eyes or the size of a person's foot," said Charley.

"That's true," said Josephine. "What's astonishing is how we found each other, considering where we came from."

25
IN WHICH The News Breaks

THE NEW YORK SUN

SCHOOL-GIRL MISSING

TUESDAY, AUGUST 12, 1884—A twelve-year-old school-girl has been reported missing by the headmistress of her school, the MacLaren Academy.

Emmeline Mary St. James was with her classmates on an excursion to Coney Island but failed to return to the railroad station with the other children.

It is believed that she is the victim of an abduction. Miss MacLaren, the chaperone in charge at the time, reports having encountered several sinister men in the holiday resort of Brooklyn.

"My girls were undertaking a study of tidal patterns in the ocean. We were not prepared for the seedy nature of the adjacent community."

Miss St. James's father, Mr. Jaffrey W. St. James, is one of the more prominent traders in this City. A hunt for the missing child has been launched by the police forces in New York City and Coney Island. Employees of the Museum of Earthly Astonishments, where the child was last seen, have been questioned at length. The reward for Miss St. James's safe return will be substantial. The punishment for those responsible will be severe.

26
IN WHICH Mr. Gideon Smyth Has an Exclusive

NEW YORK TRIBUNE

LITTLE JO-JO IN SCHOOL-GIRL SCANDAL

TUESDAY, AUGUST 12, 1884—Little Jo-Jo, this City's reigning princess of the little people, is possibly a character in the drama unfolding in Coney Island, Brooklyn, at this writing.

The schoolgirl reported missing yesterday, one Emmeline Mary St. James, was in a party from the MacLaren Academy, who were visiting R. J. Walters' famous Museum of Earthly Astonishments. Her classmates were not observing ocean tides, as the headmistress, Miss Ethelwyn MacLaren, had previously informed the press.

They traveled to the popular summer resort to seek out Little Jo-Jo, who had once been an employee in the school. It seems likely that there is a connection between the disappearance of Miss St. James and mysterious accusations against the diminutive charmer.

The headmistress claimed that Little Jo-Jo had stolen certain monies belonging to the school funds. Little Jo-Jo claimed she was mistreated at the hands of the school authorities and that the money taken was simply money owed her for unpaid wages.

Little Jo-Jo's character is so spunky and beguiling that her honesty cannot be doubted. She is a person of such appeal that her size is incidental. And there are further points of confusion in the story.

Mr. R. J. Walters asserts that he has no knowledge of any intrigue concerning his prized exhibition, despite having been present, with this reporter, at the confrontation between the volatile schoolmarm and Little Jo-Jo.

Miss MacLaren refused to respond to queries.

According to Miss Charlotte Montgomery and Miss Felicia Hicks, classmates to Miss St. James at MacLaren Academy, their headmistress had expressed annoyance that Little Jo-Jo was working for the second-rate Mr. Walters. "She thought P. T. Barnum would pay a better price to own such a freak," they declared, in an interview at the school gates yesterday.

They also suggested that the missing girl, known as Emmy, was not a likely candidate for abduction. "No one would want her," asserted Miss Hicks. "Little Jo-Jo was her only friend, but that was a secret too. No one makes friends with servants."

A city-wide search has been ordered, involving more than half the police force. Mr. Jaffrey W. St. James, father of the missing girl, has offered a reward of $200 for the safe return of his beloved daughter.

27
IN WHICH Miss MacLaren Tries Again

Josephine said good-bye to Emmy with her heart as heavy as a bucket of stones. Emmy blubbered without shame.

"Oh, Jo!"

"Dear Emmy!"

Josephine's face was pressed against Emmy's leg for a final embrace, holding back her own tears.

"I know Margaret will look after me," sobbed Emmy. "When she hears the whole story, she won't let me go back to school; she'll talk to my father, I'm certain of it."

"I know you'll be fine," whispered Josephine. "Even if you look ridiculous!"

Police constables on the lookout for Emmeline St. James, twelve-year-old school-girl, were flocking the street corners of Coney Island. Charley had insisted that a disguise was Emmy's only chance.

She was wearing Charley's second pair of trousers, though she couldn't close the buttons all the way. Her shirt had once belonged to Hilda Viemeister's brother, and her hair was scrunched into an old cap. Charley had suggested lopping off her braids with the poultry shears, but Emmy swore her mother would die, so she wore the cap instead.

Charley clapped her shoulder as if she were a real boy. "Keep your feathers fluffy," he whispered.

Nelly led Emmy away, down the street toward the train station. Josephine and Charley waved until they were out of sight.

"Let's go to the museum." Josephine longed for a distraction from the sudden hole made by Emmy's departure.

"Why go so early? We'll be in that cave long enough."

"We could walk along the beach way. We could wade in the ocean."

"You start ahead. I'll catch up when I've found my umbrella."

Josephine set off on the same path she had taken the night before. She could hear the roar of the waves, sounding like an endless wind blowing over dry grass, as soon as she left the busy concourse.

The peace of the morning was like a breath being held until it could exhale into a rowdy afternoon. Then the beach would come alive with splashing and laughter and ballyhoos of all kind, with folks selling anything that other folk might buy.

The pier was the only busy place this early in the day. The first ferry had just arrived from the city, spilling early arrivals armed with picnic baskets onto the iron-railed walkway that led to the esplanade. A buzzing chatter floated above the rolling water, anticipating a day of pleasure.

As she crouched at the edge of the sand to remove her boots and stockings, Josephine glanced behind to see if Charley was in sight. Instead, something swooped down upon her, stuffing a rag into her surprised mouth, as she was knocked to the ground. Was it Mr. Walters again? Rough fabric covered her eyes in an instant, and powerful hands shoved her while wrapping her whole body tightly. He was smothering her! Her howl was trapped behind wadding already sodden with saliva.

Within seconds, swaddled in scratchy sacking, she was heaved from the ground and swung to and fro like an ordinary bundle of rags. She was helpless and gagging. One bare foot dangled free and began to kick with all its constricted might. She was dropped at once onto the sand, then felt hands fiercely shaking her.

"Do not think for a minute that you will escape me." The whispered voice was all too recognizable. "You're mine now, and I'll sell you to the highest bidder!"

Miss MacLaren had reclaimed her prize.

What did she mean—sell? What bidders? Like a choice pig at auction! Was she really worth so much that grown-ups would behave this way?

Josephine was lifted again, her arms twisted and her legs crunched up tightly in a knot. Her cheek and brow pressed against the web of the sacking. Her nose seemed full of tiny fibers. Trying to breathe through her mouth was like sucking cotton.

Miss MacLaren was already wheezing slightly, struggling with Josephine's nineteen pounds. If she would only collapse with a heart attack! With that in mind, Josephine squirmed harder.

"Hey!" A distant call. "What have you got there?" It was Charley!

Miss MacLaren, grunting, tucked her parcel clumsily under one arm and tried to trot.

"Hey! I've found Jo's shoes here! Hey! You! Come back here!"

Josephine's stomach reeled with Miss MacLaren's unsteady sway. The sand beneath city shoes seemed to be an obstacle. Charley would surely catch up. Where were they headed? Josephine was going to be sick, she knew it. Miss MacLaren's body smelled of custard gone sour in the sun. Each lurch crushed Josephine's nose closer to the source.

Suddenly the footing changed. They were clattering upward on something that chimed under shoes. It was the ramp to the New Iron Pier! Miss MacLaren meant to take her back to the city on the ferry!

Every step took her farther from Charley. Josephine tried to thrash and was promptly pinched. She could hear the lilting calls of boys selling ices and roasted potatoes. The pier must be more crowded than the beach; they seemed to be dodging people. Charley would lose sight of them! Josephine strained to see through the weave of the sacking.

"Excuse me, young man!" Miss MacLaren was nearly breathless. Josephine felt blood rush to her face as her captor stumbled.

"Do you have a ticket, ma'am?" They were at the gangplank! The voice was so close it made Josephine twitch. Was this really the way things were going to end? Her mouth was dry and full of bits of hemp.

"Yes, yes, here it is. But sir, that frightening hooligan back there has been following me. Please be sure he does not board the ferry."

"Yes'm. Join the line over there. Folks is boarding now."

"Thank you. Watch that boy."

Josephine listened with dread. What chance did she have? What could she do? Miss MacLaren was moving again, up the gangplank, onto the boat's deck, taking short, wobbling steps. Her breaths were like little piggy grunts.

"Hey, you there!" the ticket taker was shouting at Charley. "Off the ramp, boy! You're not wanted here!"

"Josephine!" She heard Charley's voice ring out. "Jo! I'm coming right back! I'll get the police! I'll get Mr. Walters! We'll be right back to save you!"

"Get off with you, you ugly ghoul!" The ticket man was not impressed.

Josephine managed to turn her neck enough to spit

out the rag. She ran her tongue back and forth across dry lips.

"Help!" she cried weakly. "Help me!"

Miss MacLaren came to an instant stop. Josephine was shifted and squeezed with vicious intent. Tears sprang to her eyes as she yelped in pain. Her curls were now tangled in the webbing of the bag and were yanked till her scalp burned.

"If you so much as breathe before this ferry leaves the slip," Miss MacLaren's threat was spoken in a strangled whisper, "I swear, I will shave your head and sell you as a bald monkey."

Josephine was once again dropped to the ground. This time, she landed not on soft sand, but on the rigid boat deck. Her body bounced, and bruised, but she swallowed her cry. She stopped breathing, and felt the distant hum of the boat's steam engine as it fired up to go. Ever so slightly, Josephine could feel the roll of the ocean far beneath her.

Miss MacLaren's thick ankles stood like soldiers, pressing in on either side of her. Josephine knew that she lay in the shadow of the woman's skirt. She could also tell, for the first time, that there was nothing tying the sack in place. It had been Miss MacLaren's hands or arm alone that had restrained her.

Slowly Josephine inched her legs out of their curled position. When her toes felt air, she paused. Now what? Could she possibly get away?

"Jo!" She heard Charley call her name, just as the

boat's whistle blew a tremendous, foggy blast. The deck under her shoulders seemed to shiver as the boat pre-pared to move.

Miss MacLaren turned quickly, shifting her feet away from their guard duty. This was Josephine's chance. She scrambled out with a whoop and a growl. She tore the sack from her head, ripping out the few hairs still caught inside. Her eyes blazed. Her fingers clenched like talons as she faced Miss MacLaren. The row of ferry riders crackled with sudden interest.

Miss MacLaren lunged at her, cussing like a sailor. A murmur of dismay arose on all sides, and ladies turned discreetly aside. Josephine jumped back a pace, ready to dart away.

"Is this your child, Madam?"

From behind her, the well-meant question acted as a catapult for Josephine. In two seconds, she had climbed the iron railing and hesitated on the top rung, staring down into the water that foamed around the bow of the boat.

"You hideous, ungrateful freak!" Miss MacLaren hollered.

"Charley?" cried Josephine, searching the faces on the pier, only an arm's length away.

"Jo? Where are you?" He had pushed through to the front row, but now was squinting in confusion.

"I'm here, Charley! I'm here!" Josephine saw his white hair shining. She saw his pale arms stretched toward her.

"Catch me, Charley!"

Josephine leaned out, and her fingers grazed
Charley's as the boat pulled away, propelling Josephine
into the air. Her skirt ballooned around her as she
pitched into the ocean.

28
Josephine Recovers

The appalled wail of the onlookers was
drowned out by the churning sound of surf
under water. Josephine plunged below the waves, holding her breath without planning to, without even knowing she should. The cold, the wet, the surprise slapped
away her desperation. Just when she needed air again,
her tiny body was thrust to the surface and stayed there,
bobbing like a seagull.

An excited clamor broke out on the pier.

"She's up! She's alive!"

"Jo!"

Someone threw a rope, but it hung short and didn't
quite reach her. Her dress floated on the surface around
her, keeping her up instead of dragging her down. No
one could reach her for some time. She knew they were
calling to her, but she was enthralled with the salty,
buoyant water and didn't try to answer.

Josephine drifted under the pier, where she was in peril of collision with the pylons holding it up. She began to kick, but the motion tangled her dress and she lost her calm. As she tried to call out between mouthfuls, she was seized by the eager hands of a passing swimmer. He towed her to the beach, murmuring assurances in Italian the whole way.

Josephine was shivering, perhaps more from the shock than the cold. When she arrived on the sand, her legs wouldn't hold her upright. Charley sprinted the length of the New Iron Pier, pausing to swipe a towel from the Ravenhall Bathing Palace. He wrapped her up like a baby and carried her home.

Hilda Viemeister collected every blanket in the house and piled them on top of Josephine, until nothing more could be seen than a pair of green eyes and a mop of damp hair. Hilda brewed beef tea and Charley fed it to Josephine by spoon.

"Uck! It's poison! And I'm not sick! Just shivery, is all."

Charley spied from the top of the stairs when Hilda answered a sharp knock at the door.

"Good afternoon, Ma'am. The name is Police Constable Vincent Beale, Ma'am. I'm inquiring after the health of the little lady?"

"She's terrible poorly, Constable, she won't be answering any questions today. Now, be off with you, please!"

It was several hours before Nelly got back from taking Emmy to the city. She had expected them all to be working, of course. She told Josephine that when she arrived at the museum, the earnest Officer Beale was soothing an irate Mr. Walters with facts of the incident as far as he knew them, which wasn't very far.

Within minutes, Nelly was running full speed to the boarding house, causing quite a stir on the concourse as she picked up her skirts and revealed strong, galloping legs to the morning shoppers. Nelly sent Charley off to report to Mr. Walters, while she sat on Josephine's bed, stroking the wee forehead and smoothing down her hair.

Josephine wondered how such a thing as fingers could feel so full of love, and she promptly burst into tears. Nelly lay down next to her and listened while she gulped and shook and sobbed.

Finally calm, Josephine told Nelly everything, from the moment onstage when she had first seen Miss MacLaren, to the dreadful hour in Marco's cage, to the view from the railing of the steamer ferry.

"I thought Charley could see me, I thought we were closer. I'd jump, and he'd catch me. Then the boat moved, and I fell straight in."

"You were brave," said Nelly.

"No, I was desperate. Brave is when I go talk to Mr. Walters. I can't work there anymore, Nelly. But what else can I do?"

"Folks like you and Charley aren't welcome just any-where, but I suppose we could find another place where the two of you can be who you are."

The word "we" meant more to Josephine than she could say. She blinked hard to stop from crying again.

Nelly pulled the blankets straight. "You need to be sleeping now. Close your eyes and think of where you might like to be sailing to in your dreams."

The following morning brought more visitors to Hilda Viemeister's door.

Mr. R. J. Walters brought a jar of clam chowder from the chowder wagon, and bottles of root beer, but he was not permitted to see Josephine.

"She's got plenty more resting to do before you'll see her again," Hilda Viemeister told him, while Josephine and Charley swallowed giggles upstairs.

After work, Charley brought home a nosegay of daisies from Filipe and a picture card bearing Best Wishes from Eddie and Rosie. Mr. Gideon Smyth deliv-ered a box of chocolates tied with a velvet ribbon, with a letter requesting an interview at her convenience.

Josephine and Charley ate the chocolates all in one evening, after allowing Nelly and Hilda to make their selections. After the first day, Josephine was not poorly at all. She had never felt better.

The first news of Miss MacLaren's fate came in a note from Emmy:

Hester Street
August 17, 1884

Dearest Josephine,

I wanted to tell you I arrived safely. Margaret's not angry with me, not even a little, she knows about running away. Where she lives with My Bob is dreadful, dreary and damp like a dungeon, and so smelly. I wrote a letter to Papa, and when he saw Margaret's sink, down the hall, shared with twelve families, he nearly fainted like a woman. He blamed My Bob, but that's not fair, everyone lives squeezed together this way, the next-door family has seven children in the same two rooms, rolling cigars all day to have money for milk. Margaret and My Bob are rich next to them.

Oh, and the tears that flowed when Papa brought us home in the carriage! Mama flung her arms around Margaret and did not let go until Jilly served the sherry. Mama said she would only forgive My Bob if they lived with us now. Papa says he will pay Margaret to be my governess and My Bob as music instructor. (My Bob says he will sneak out to play at the Half-Dollar Saloon, because that's real music, not hymns.)

When it came time for me to tell my adventure, Mama began to blubber all over again. Even Papa pretended to have a pebble of soot from the fire lodged in his eye. Mama said she hadn't slept for one minute while I was lost, and if she'd known I was with circus folk she would have slept less.

I told Papa that you saved my life, because of you I got courage. He says you could live with us too, that you could be my companion and learn school with me. Would you do that? I never had a friend until you. We have a very fine house, and no worries. MacLaren Academy will be closed, Papa is having the accounts looked at, she will be sorry.

Write to me.

God Bless, your friend,
Emmy

"That'll be something to consider, Jo," said Nelly. "Not many children in the world get offered such comfortable prospects."

"Do you think that Emmy is very rich, Nelly?" asked Josephine.

"Richer in money than you or I could ever guess, Jo. But likely, parts of Emmy's life feel poor to her."

Josephine already knew, as she folded the letter, that her future would not be as companion to Emmy St. James, however much she loved her.

Further news of Miss MacLaren arrived through Nelly. She came back from work just bursting with it.

"Set yourselves down! I've such news as you wouldn't guess till a month of Sundays has gone by." She was grinning all over her face. She had stayed late, to polish the glass display cases as she did once a week.

Josephine and Charley were already tucking in to Hilda's clam pie.

"What is it, Mumsy?" asked Charley. They could both tell it was something big.

"The reason Mr. Walters wasn't there today—"

"I was just telling Jo, he was off this morning dressed like a dandy—"

"The reason he went into the city today was to attend the hearing of Miss Ethelwyn MacLaren at the court-house. Constable Beale advised him of the time."

"And?"

"What happened, Nelly?"

Nelly's eyebrows twitched, and she imitated Mr. Walters's voice. "The judge ruled that Miss MacLaren be confined while awaiting trial. The school will be closed pending an investigation. And then—"

Nelly's voice now tightened with glee. "Mr. Walters asked special permission to address the judge, in the name of civic duty, saying that he could offer a program of hard labor to assist the prisoner's rehabilitation!"

"But what does that mean?"

"It means that Miss Ethelwyn MacLaren will be cleaning the cage of the Genuine Hippopotamus every day for a year!"

Well, Charley and Josephine laughed about that until they got the hiccups. Hilda cleared away the supper for fear they would choke.

29
IN WHICH Josephine Talks to Mr. Walters

The day arrived that Josephine had to return to the Museum of Earthly Astonishments.

She walked with the O'Dooleys in the morning, as if she were going to work like any other day of the summer. She wore her green linen dress, which Nelly had laundered and carefully pressed after its dunk in the salt water. Sadly, somewhere along the sand during his chase after Miss MacLaren, Charley had dropped one of Josephine's custom-made buckled shoes out of his pocket. She was back to wearing her oversized lace-ups, with balls of newspaper in the toes.

The sky was sheeted in cloud, with no hint of blue. They avoided the beach, and stayed on Surf Avenue. The hoopla of the day was just beginning. Vendors vied for position with their wagons, and the smell of their wares vied for first place too. Sausages cooking, clams frying, chowder warming, waffles crisping, corn-on-the-cob steaming.

Charley was already ready for lunch when he'd just finished breakfast. They turned up 8th Street to reach the museum.

"I'll come with you to find Mr. Walters," offered Nelly.

"Charley can watch the door for a bit. There aren't so many people here in the morning."

"No, Nelly, but thank you." Josephine knew she had to meet with him alone.

As she passed through the main promenade, Josephine greeted Rosie and Eddie with true affection. She even scratched Marco's belly when she said hello to Filipe.

"Don't get too friendly." Charley laughed at her side. "I'm sure he'd still like a wee nibble out of you."

"It's as though I've been away three months instead of just three days," sighed Josephine, glancing around at all the familiar props. The chair on her platform looked forlorn, like a plump spinster awaiting an invitation to dance.

"Did you see the new Curiosity?" Charley spoke quietly. "I didn't like to mention it before."

Josephine followed him to the glass case. He lifted her high enough to peek in, to see her own pearl-studded Mary Lincoln shoes, sitting between Paddy Parker's handcuffs and the horn of an African Rhinoceros. The card, hand-lettered in Mr. Walters's fine script, read:

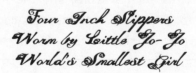

Four Inch Slippers
Worn by Little Jo-Jo
World's Smallest Girl

Josephine felt a shiver race up her neck.

"Is he saying he knows I'm leaving? That I won't be needing those slippers anymore?"

Charley shrugged.

Does he know that it's his own fault anyway, for being so callous, she thought silently. Every time she remembered Mr. Walters pushing her into the cage, she got hot about the ears.

"Jo, he's not a bad man. And he's been kind to you, like it or not to recall."

"I do remember, the very first night, how he tucked his handkerchief into my collar while I ate my bacon and potatoes, as if my raggedy dress was something to be protected."

"You see? Not all bad. Now, go and get it done with, before you change your mind."

Charley went off to find his cravat.

Josephine watched him, thinking of the journey to meet Charley for the first time, sitting astride Mr. Walters's shoulders, with her hands folded on his silky top hat.

She paused in her own dressing room. Barker shambled over and nosed her gently. She ruffled his fur and tugged on his ears the way he liked. His tongue swiped her face like a wet cloth. She pulled back, laughing, drying her cheek with the back of her hand. She would miss old Barker.

But she was avoiding what she was here to do. She took a deep breath and sauntered down the corridor as if she had nothing more in mind than a how-de-do. She found Mr. Walters in the performance tent, behind the museum. He was examining the curtain where it was worn right through.

He stood up straight when he saw Josephine, towering above her.

"I've been wondering when you might find time to come around to see your benefactor."

"Thank you for the chowder and the root beer, Mr. Walters." Josephine stretched her neck back to see his face. It was hard to begin her speech.

"And thank you, uh, thank you also for the opportunity of being Little Jo-Jo." She stopped. Mr. Walters had arched one eyebrow.

"But," she went on in a hurry, "if being Little Jo-Jo means getting stuffed in a cage like a pickpocket, well, I'll be Josephine from now on."

Mr. Walters sat down, his legs dangling over the edge of the stage. He patted the floor next to him, but Josephine stayed where she was.

Mr. Walters sighed.

"Josephine," he began. "I am compelled to adjust your thinking."

Josephine folded her arms across her chest and quietly tapped her foot.

"You missed an appearance," he said, ignoring her glare. "It is not permissible to miss an appearance."

Josephine tapped her foot more quickly.

"I have every right to keep things running smoothly on the premises, using whatever method is required." His manner was cool, but he watched her closely, as if waiting for something.

She could not remember the words she had practiced.

"Well, it wasn't nice, is all." Josephine faltered. It wasn't nice. But Mr. Walters would never see that it was wicked either. To him, it was business and nothing more. "What I mean is, I can't be Little Jo-Jo anymore."

Mr. Walters sighed a second time and shook his head back and forth.

"We have an arrangement, Josephine. I paid off your debt to that ridiculous schoolteacher. There can be no question that you work for me. There are painted advertisements all over the resort, enticing people through the museum doors to see you."

"I don't think people will be too happy, sir, paying to see Little Jo-Jo in a cage. Because that's where you'll have to keep me, screaming and scratching in a cage. I don't want to work here anymore." She could feel the cage around her as she spoke, making the skin on her arms prickle with gooseflesh.

"Is that the trouble? The cage?" He used his warmest voice. "Ah, Josephine. Perhaps the cage was a mistake."

"Perhaps?"

"The cage was a mistake. It was expedient. I do not like being crossed, and the punishment was at hand. But I was protecting you too, from the bellowing harridan. Remember that."

Mr. Walters extended his arm, but Josephine pretended not to see. He withdrew his hand.

"If you choose not to repair the rent, Josephine, you will wear a shabby coat."

"I just think it's time for me to leave, is all."

"Do we have to go over this again, Josephine?" Irritation clipped his words. "I made an enormous investment in you—"

"Are you trying to flimflam me, Mr. Walters? Didn't you make your money back that you spent on me? The clothes and shoes added up together couldn't be more than a week's admission prices, the crowds we've been getting all summer."

"As a matter of fact," said Mr. Walters, "the take at the door has subsided considerably in recent weeks."

Josephine knew that wasn't true. She'd been there every day except the last three, and the hall was always full.

"I'm pretty fair at calculation, and I don't think you've been cheated out of your investment."

"We'll be heading back to the city soon," said Mr. Walters. "There are always extra expenses at moving time."

"I'm not feeling sorry for you, sir. You've made plenty more dollars than I have this summer."

And she'd done just fine, she reminded herself. "But the master is always better paid than the servant; I'm not complaining. I'm used to that."

She smiled at him, wanting to convince him now.

"I do think you deserve it," she added, finally sitting down a few feet away from him. "You hired me to change your fortune, and I'm glad that I did."

He glanced at her with suspicion.

"Only now it's time to make my own fortune."

"You're not so much of a novelty anymore, Josephine. People lose interest after a while. Who cares to pay twice to gawp at the same thing?"

"I'll go far away, where people haven't seen me yet."

Mr. Walters acted as though he wasn't listening. He shrugged his enormous shoulders and spoke to his own hands. "I've been looking for a new act anyway. I've hired a family of Eskimos to join the museum in the autumn. As soon as I can keep ice for more than an hour at a time."

"Oh, Mr. Walters!" He looked tired to her, with smudges beneath his dark eyes. She didn't want to tell him the next part.

"You won't like this," she said quietly, "but Nelly and Charley are coming with me."

"What!?"

Josephine watched him, finding that she didn't like to hurt him.

"It's time for all of us to move along." It came out in a whisper.

Mr. Walters gazed at her, slowly running his fingertips along his grand moustache. Finally, he reached into his pocket and pulled out the folding measuring stick.

"I did warn you," he said in a steady voice, "that if you grew, I would consider your contract terminated." He held the stick straight against her back.

"I don't think I grew in inches, Mr. Walters." Though

certainly she'd grown in what she knew about things.

"On the contrary." Mr. Walters refolded the stick. "You are nearly twenty-nine inches," he announced.

"That's it, then," agreed Josephine, suddenly understanding. "I've grown."

Mr. Walters reached out and shook her small hand, like a businessman closing a deal.

"Josephine? You may as well take your dresses with you. They won't fit anyone else."

He was trying to bestow a gift. He was trying to apologize.

She smiled at him, aiming for his hidden heart. For less than a moment he smiled back. Then he shook his head, as if catching himself from going soft.

"On second thought," he said gruffly, "you may choose just one of them. The others will make a charming exhibit, set up on a plaster model just your size."

30

IN WHICH **Mr. Gideon Smyth Says Good-bye**

NEW YORK TRIBUNE

LITTLE JO-JO DEPARTS MUSEUM

AUGUST 24, 1884—Little Jo-Jo, the celebrated Lilliputian star of R. J. Walters' Museum of Earthly Astonishments, has departed from her position there, with little explanation.

The petite charmer was discovered by Mr. Walters last spring and performed daily throughout most of the summer.

As reported in the *New York Tribune*, she was the victim recently of an attempted abduction. A former employer, Miss Ethelwyn MacLaren, has been charged in that crime.

It comes as no surprise that the spirited Little Jo-Jo should wish to improve her circumstances. Her admirable character and appealing visage will be welcome in fine parlors and theatrical venues wherever she goes. The cultural population of this City will miss her. We wish her well.

Epilogue

S.S. Fair Britannia
September 9, 1884

Dear dear Emmy,

You might laugh if you saw me, wrapped in a blanket on what the sailors call a deck-chair. That means a chair that sits on the deck. The sailors never sit down, but I do. When I try to walk, I am toppled over in an instant. Even this ship, as big as a cathedral, is not so steady against the ocean swell. I am the size of a gargoyle.

When I opened the tidy package you wrapped and found the new shoes inside, I about swooned. You couldn't choose a better thing to make me remember you every day of our travels. I could say "Thank you" till sunset, which takes a long time on the ocean.

With all the dollars I saved this summer, I paid my own passage for the voyage. And Nelly is still pinching

*herself that your father insisted on giving her the
reward for your safe return. I told her what you said,
that having her help change things was the same as
saving your life. So she deserves the dollars. And now
she and Charley are here with me, having a grand time.*

*We had supper last night at the captain's table. We
were told it was an honor, but he slurped his soup as
noisy as old Barker.*

*We are giddy like children, thinking about all the
sights ahead of us. I wish you could be here too. But
we'll tell you all the stories when we come home again.*

> *Your friend,*
> *Josephine*

*P.S. Charley sends a hello and says to keep your
feathers fluffy.*

Josephine first appeared in my imagination as a magical person, even smaller than she is in the book. I soon realized that I wanted her to be a real child who faced the world from a different perspective than most of us do. Although her troubles are often the result of her size, her solutions come from quick wits and courage, qualities available to all of us.

Mr. P. T. Barnum and his most famous midget exhibits, General Tom Thumb and Lavinia Bump Warren, are the only real people in this book. All the other characters I made up to help tell a story about a time and place in American history that always have fascinated me.

Josephine is not real either, but she has a real condition, which is now known as dwarfism. It was P. T. Barnum who coined the word *midget*. Today people like Josephine prefer to be called a short-statured person or Little Person.

The Museum of Earthly Astonishments did not exist, but there were dozens of real "dime museums" in the New York area during the second half of the nineteenth century. Mr. Walters was like many curators who displayed all of the "curiosities" mentioned in the story, as well as many more, human and otherwise.

In 1884, when *Earthly Astonishments* takes place, Coney Island was beginning to be a popular resort for New Yorkers. The steamer ferry and new railway lines encouraged thousands of day-trippers to come and spend their hard-earned dollars on a holiday by the sea.

Within twenty years, Coney Island became the home of three racetracks, several huge hotels, and three spectacular amusement parks. One of the most exotic attractions was an entire miniature city housing 300 midgets, whose whole lives were a performance for the gawking crowds. I made Josephine sail away before she could be a part of that.

The first roller coaster was invented the summer that Josephine lived in Coney Island, but she and Charley did not have a chance to ride it. It consisted of a wooden cart that rattled down a hill of railway track and then back up another incline, where it came to a stop.

Until 1918, United States law did not compel children to go to school. Wealthy children mostly did, and poor children mostly didn't. Poor children, from the age of seven or eight, often worked to help provide for their families, in any number of jobs that Charley was happy to avoid: factory labor, shoe-shining, rolling cigars, or newspaper selling. There were also thousands of children, as Josephine saw, who had no families and lived on the streets.

During the 1880s, the section of New York City now known as the Lower East Side was one of the most crowded places on earth. Over a million people, including many immigrants from Europe and Ireland and China, lived within just a few blocks, crammed into dark, airless, filthy tenement buildings. Often two or three families shared one apartment, as Nelly and Charley did with the Wongs, making do with primitive plumbing and straw beds.

For Emmy's sister, Margaret, coming from a privileged home,

the poverty and squalor would have been a shock. Nelly and Margaret probably earned only a couple of dollars a week. Out of that they would have had to pay for rent and food, clothing, and household supplies. There would certainly be nothing left over for treats.

Josephine's proud gesture of buying her own dress and shoes would have used up her five precious dollars, but not much more. Certainly her wages from Mr. Walters, on top of her room and board, would allow her the luxury of savings!

Although there continue to be Little People working with carnivals and circuses, they are there by their own choice. Human beings will always be curious about those who are different from themselves, but it is up to each of us not to be cruel.